Binny
Bewitched

Also by Hilary McKay

Binny
Bewitched

Hilary McKay

Margaret K. McElderry Books

New York   London   Toronto   Sydney   New Delhi

MARGARET K. McELDERRY BOOKS
An imprint of Simon & Schuster Children's Publishing Division
1230 Avenue of the Americas, New York, New York 10020
This book is a work of fiction. Any references to historical events, real people, or real places are used fictitiously. Other names, characters, places, and events are products of the author's imagination, and any resemblance to actual events or places or persons, living or dead, is entirely coincidental.
Text copyright © 2017 by Hilary McKay
Illustrations copyright © 2017 by Tony Ross
Published by arrangement with Hodder Children's Books,
a division of Hachette Children's Books
First published in Great Britain in 2016 by Hodder Children's Books
First U.S. Edition, 2017
All rights reserved, including the right
of reproduction in whole or in part in any form.
MARGARET K. McELDERRY BOOKS
is a trademark of Simon & Schuster, Inc.
For information about special discounts for bulk purchases,
please contact Simon & Schuster Special Sales at 1-866-506-1949
or business@simonandschuster.com.
The Simon & Schuster Speakers Bureau can bring authors
to your live event. For more information or to book an event,
contact the Simon & Schuster Speakers Bureau at 1-866-248-3049
or visit our website at www.simonspeakers.com.
Also available in a Margaret K. McElderry Books hardcover edition
Cover design by Lauren Rille
Book design by Tom Daly
The text for this book was set in Excelsior.
The illustrations for this book were rendered in pen and ink wash.
Manufactured in the United States of America
0518 OFF
First Margaret K. McElderry Books paperback edition June 2018
2 4 6 8 10 9 7 5 3 1
CIP data for this book is available from the Library of Congress.
ISBN 978-1-4814-9102-0 (hc)
ISBN 978-1-4814-9103-7 (pbk)
ISBN 978-1-4814-9104-4 (eBook)

For Anne McNeil, with love and thanks,

Hilary

Chapter One

* * *

Binny in Trouble

From the New Notebook

We have been unpacking the last few boxes of things from our old house. It is four years since they were packed. Mum remembers that Granny did it when Dad died and we had to move. Granny is dead now too.

There are a lot of dead people in my family.

How sad that looks, written down. I tried it on my friends, first Gareth and then Clare.

Gareth said, "There are a lot of dead people in everyone's families. There are more live ones in your family than mine."

A short arguing calculation proved that he was right. Gareth is an only child and he does not count his wicked stepmother as family because she is allergic to dogs, although otherwise not wicked at all.

Clare was just as unsympathetic. She said, "Old people are meant to be dead."

"Dad wasn't really old. Not ancient old, like Granny."

"If we are going to start moaning about fathers," said Clare, "get ready to get over yourself because I will win."

Clare's father disappeared when she was six weeks old, remarking (as he dumped two children and one small unprofitable farm on Clare's mother) (but took the family car) that he could do without the stress. Clare says he owes her twelve birthday presents, thirteen Christmas presents, thirteen Easter eggs, eight good excuses for missing school sports day, and fifteen parents' evenings. So she is right, she will win, and anyway, I was not moaning. I was just trying out what I had written in my notebook against real life. I said this to Clare, and she replied, "There shouldn't be any difference," and I couldn't be bothered to explain to her that she was wrong.

But I didn't mean to sound sad when I wrote about my family. We are not sad.

Not even about money.

I wish we had more money.

Before my father died my family didn't have to worry about money. Or anyway, we thought we didn't. But we were wrong, and so we went bankrupt, Mum and

Clem and James and me, but not Dad, he died just in time. What I mean is, if you have to die, it's better to do it before you go bankrupt. And have to sell your family bookshop and your house and lose your dog Max and go and live in dingy little flats where the damp gives you coughs and there is no outside space and all the people you thought were your friends turn out not to care much about you after all.

And you turn out not to care much about them. You haven't time. You hang on tight and forget a lot of things.

We forgot the boxes. They were at Granny's house for ages. Then we moved here, to Cornwall, and the boxes came with us but they still didn't get unpacked. That was because we were too busy getting rid of the ten thousand bags of junk and ten million spiders left behind by Aunty Violet, whose house this used to be.

It wasn't box-time then, either. Just when we had it possible to live here without something making you scream or falling down on you, an autumn gale swept in from the sea and blew great holes in the roof.

When you have a roof, you don't think about it. But when you don't have a roof, when you go up the stairs in your house and see your bedroom and your soggy wallpaper and your school shoes filled with rain, and sky over your head, proper sky, real sky with clouds and airplanes, a lot of sky, then you think about roofs.

The roof only took a few hours to blow off, but it took

months to get back on again. When it was on, but the scaffolding was still there, I climbed up and I leaned right over the new tiles and I pushed and pulled as hard as I could. I was checking that nothing was loose. Pete, the builder who had done the tiling, saw me and came up and grabbed me by my jacket and he made me put an orange hard hat on and he didn't let go until he got me on the ground. Then he shouted a lot, and he said he would tell my mother and he did.

So I was officially told off and made to promise not to do it again. It wasn't a very good telling off, not good enough for Pete, because Mum admitted she'd been wondering about doing the same thing herself.

"At least now we know it's solid," she said, hugging me, and Clem and James were also pleased to hear how tightly our new roof was stuck on.

"It didn't move, even a tiny bit?" asked James.

"Of course it flipping didn't move even a tiny bit!" said Pete. "Don't you trust me?"

"Oh yes," said James, and Mum and Clem agreed, "Oh yes, oh yes," and then Clem asked how high I'd managed to reach, and Mum wanted to know if I'd tried in more than one place, and if I'd seen any cracks.

"Well, thank you very much!" said Pete, and he stalked off in a huff.

(My writing has gone wandering away. It has left

the boxes, still unpacked, and ended up on the roof of our house.)

So back to the boxes.

One of them was very heavy. It was full of great big albums. The largest, labeled "Clemency's First Year," was stuffed with photos and excited comments like: First taste of APPLE!!!! and HOW did Clemency get RIGHT to the end of her cot??? (There were four of these: spring, summer, autumn, and winter.) I just got one album, half full, and poor old James had a completely empty-except-for-the-first-page scrapbook. He was not happy about this and wanted Mum to sit down and write four more volumes instantly.

"I will, I will," said Mum, "or you can have a giant bag of Mexican Barbecue Fries. They were on sale. Go and look in the cupboard!"

As well as the albums there were boxes of storybooks from when we were little, and from when Mum and Dad were little too, and there was Dad's old brown bag.

How strange to see that bag, so familiar and so forgotten. I knew every mark and scuff on the leather, but I had never looked inside. Dad never went out of the house without it. The handle was shaped from years and years of being held in the grip of his right hand.

"Are we going to open it?" asked Clem.

Mum said she would rather not just then, but that Clem and I could if we liked. We nearly didn't; it had been shut for so long. We looked at it for ages before we undid the buckle. It felt so wrong. I wondered if Clem felt as I did, that perhaps in the bag would be something to help us understand why he had left so suddenly and unhelpfully, like someone walking out in the middle of a conversation.

There is a book called The Railway Children that we found when we were unpacking the boxes and in it there is a family with a father who goes away. The eldest girl, who is called Bobby, doesn't know where he's gone, and she says IS HE DEAD? but he's not. He's in prison.

Dad went bankrupt. Do you get put in prison for that?

There is a stupid thought that I used to let myself think. It begins, What If . . . ?

I didn't go to Dad's funeral. Clem and James did, but not me. I can't remember one thing about it, but I have been told that at the last minute I went out with our next-door neighbor instead. I have been told that she heroically took me to McDonald's, which she chose because she supposed the staff there were used to children behaving terribly. And so they were and so I did, and when the staff heard why we were there, and where we really should have been, the heroic neighbor was given free coffee and tissues and I was given unlimited access to the ice-cream machine, the M&M's dispenser, and the tap that squirts tomato sauce.

I missed the funeral, but it still happened. I know that. I know how unreasonable it is to think, *What If . . . ?* I hardly ever do it anymore. But what if Dad is in prison, not dead? Then we really shouldn't look inside his bag.

I was thinking this when Clem, who had been very quiet, said "Well," and sighed and began undoing the buckle.

What had Dad been thinking of, when he closed his bag for the last time?

He had been thinking about us.

Dad died the week before Clem's birthday. I don't think she had one that year, not one that we noticed, anyway. But Dad had not forgotten. The first thing we saw when we looked inside his bag was a little package with a label, a birthday present for Clem. It was all wrapped up with a birthday card for when she was thirteen. A silvery charm bracelet with three charms: music notes and a silver flute and a C for Clem with the C a crescent moon and a crystal like a star. Always on birthdays Dad used to buy extra presents for non birthday people and they were in the bag too. An engine driver's hat for James, and a very loud whistle to blow when the train was ready to leave the station (because when he was three James was obsessed with trains).

A thick blue notebook for me with silver writing in French on the cover under a silver sketch from Dad's favorite book, The Little Prince. The card with it said, "With love from Daddy. Never stop writing!"

In the picture on the cover the Little Prince is leaving his very small planet with a flock of birds to help him fly. He is leaving his rose and his sheep and his active volcano. Dad used to call me his active volcano sometimes, and once I asked him, "And is Clem the rose? And James the sheep?"

But he had said, no. He said I was the rose and the sheep and the active volcano, all mixed up together. "The whole story," he said, "and the birds are your words."

I don't know how I could stop writing. I write all the time. But I have never had a book to write in as beautiful as this one. The paper is very smooth and creamy, and there is silver elastic that snaps round when it is closed to keep the words safe. The writing on the cover says, "L'essential est invisible pour les yeux."

One day I will find out what that means.

There was a pencil from our bookshop to go with the notebook, one of the pencils Dad used to give away free.

After the presents I didn't want to look anymore and neither did Clem. We didn't know what to do with the bag. *It seemed it should go in an important place, but there aren't really any important places in our house. It's too small. So in the end we put it back in the box. Mum said, "I think we'll leave it for a while."*

I know why.

To see his writing, and the pencil from the bookshop. It felt like he might step through the door.

Chapter Two

* * *

Friday Afternoon

The marketplace traders were closing their stalls. Somebody was whistling, just out of sight.

Then there was barking and a small dog raced by, trailing a scarlet leash and lifting a great rattling crowd of marketplace pigeons into flight.

A shriek of dismay and bird wings filling the air, and then concerned voices calling, all the sounds gathering together like a wave before it breaks.

Binny heard all this, but she was not part of it. She was in the same place as the pigeons and the dog and the people, but it was a completely different world. She was standing beside the bank. Its deep gray doorway arched behind her, like a sea cave. A little way in front was the ATM. Left behind at the ATM was a pile of money.

The money had a presence, like a spell, and Binny (green eyed, seaweed hair, sweater-swamped, super-market sneakers, four library books hugged tight to her chest for warmth) was spellbound to the cobbles, locked between a lamppost and the stony walls of the bank, trembling a little.

All the way across town that afternoon, Binny had ached for money. The longing to have it had pounded in her mind: *just once, just once, just this one time and I'll never want any again.*

And now, this magic.

A soft pigeon feather, white as sea foam, bubble-light, came drifting down toward the ground. Binny took two steps toward the ATM and reached out a hand.

The money was in twenty-pound notes. Purple-pinky-brownish color. They felt silky, but not smooth. Their texture was more like dry leaves than paper. Somehow that leafy feel made them very real. Binny clutched them tight, her heart banging, and nobody said, "Oy!"

The notes folded naturally into the palm of her hand. Her hand tucked itself into her jeans pocket, the left one, that didn't have a hole in it.

The feather touched the ground.

Then the little dog was recaptured and the pigeons

became quiet and Binny, with a pocketful of money, gathered as easily as a shell from the beach, continued on her journey home from school.

It was the last Friday before the half-term break. Binny was alone because her friends were at a meeting. They were being given final plans for the half-term school trip to a new adventure center, just opened in the next county. Binny was the only person in her class not going. Even Clare would be away, half paid for by her mother and brother, half earned by herself. "Try and come too," she had begged, but Binny had not even taken the letter home.

"No thanks!" she had said after reading the description: *Outdoor adventures during the day, music and theater in the evenings. The one experience you must not miss! A chance to discover who you really are! Find out how to follow your dreams!*

"Sounds boring," Binny had growled, fooling no one.

"I'm guessing," said Mr. Martin, the French teacher who was going with the group, "that it will be the first of many of these trips. So don't worry about not coming this time, Binny. Probably before long we will be heading off again."

Binny had managed a smile because she could see he meant to be kind, but she had been much more comforted when he said suddenly, "I could never go to places either when I was at school!"

"Because of money?" asked Binny.

He nodded.

"But you go to places now," said Binny, kindly. "France and places, don't you?"

"I do. So will you. But it's tough when all your friends are going."

"A bit," admitted Binny.

Her friends had talked of nothing else for days. They would come back enlightened; having discovered who they really were. Some of them, those who had an idea already (*wildlife vet, helicopter pilot, dog walker, firework technician*) would be the luckiest of all because they would find out how to follow those dreams.

"They'll be back in no time," said Mr. Martin encouragingly.

"I know. It doesn't matter. It's not the most important thing I want money for."

Mr. Martin laughed and said, "When I think of the shopping list I used to have! Got anything interesting planned this weekend?"

"It's Mum's birthday."

"Is that the most important thing?"

"Yes."

"Ah!" said Mr. Martin. "Yes of course, *bien entendu!* That means I completely understand!"

Bien entendu! thought Binny, with pleasure, because it was sometimes nice to be completely understood.

Even so, she walked home longing for money. It

is, she thought, *bien entendu* that you should have a proper birthday present for your mother.

And now she could. Her wishes had come true. It had happened. A miracle.

"Thank you! Thank you!" Binny whispered aloud, to wherever the magic had come from, and she went on her way battered and buffeted and washed by waves of joy.

Chapter Three

✳ ✳ ✳

Friday Evening and Saturday Morning

Binny lived in a very small, very old house with her mother, Polly; her seventeen-year-old sister, Clem; and James, who seemed to have been six for a very long time. As well as the humans, there was Cinderella the white cat, and in the longest school vacations: Christmas, Easter, and summer, Binny and Gareth's shared dog, Max. Two hundred years before, the house had been built for a Cornish fisherman and his family. There were dozens of houses just like it in the town, with steep red roofs and white painted walls, narrow gardens behind, and front doors that opened straight onto the cobbled, narrow street. It was two minutes' walk from the market and five minutes from the harbor. A lovely place to live if you could manage with hardly any space and people glancing in through your windows all day long. Many of the little white houses had been made into vacation cottages, often joined with their next-door neighbor to make one larger house out of two small ones. But Binny's home was unchanged and her family had lived in it more or less comfortably until the night when the roof became sky.

Months later, the family finances still had not recovered from this expensive adventure. The roof had been repaired, the rain-soaked ceilings and beds replaced, but even now there was still one builder left, plastering walls and rehanging doors and doing noisy mysterious things in the attic. Since he had never quite finished, he was never quite paid, but there had been many other large bills. The children's mother had worked extra shifts at the old people's home in town and Clem had hurried from college to wait on tables in the café by the harbor. Binny had managed with no bedroom carpet and no new clothes, and recently, since she had tried to hang a hammock from it and wrenched it from its hinges, no bedroom door.

"Binny!" her mother had exclaimed, staring at the damage. "Not another thing to be mended!"

Binny had said she didn't want it to be mended, she liked having no bedroom door. "Good!" said Clem and her mother. "Under the circumstances, good!"

The circumstances, of course, were money. They all

thought about money so often and with such anxiety that it was like an extra nightmare person living in the house. Only James seemed to have escaped untroubled.

Or had he? Earlier that day, the day of the whistle and the small white dog and the pigeons and the twenty-pound notes that felt like leaves, Binny had asked, "What are you getting Mum for her birthday on Sunday?"

"A picture of me!" James had answered. "A lovely one! From school, when they took all our photographs."

"Then Mum will have to pay for it!" Binny had objected.

"No she won't. Because when they were giving them out to take home I told Miss that I didn't want mine because of the roof blowing off and now we only have bourbon creams instead of proper chocolate cookies. I said it in my sad voice, and Miss said, *Oh James!* Like that. *Oh James!* Then, guess what, then just before home time she waited till the others had gone and whispered I could have it for free! And . . ." James had paused, making round eyes at Binny. "She gave me her Kit Kat from her lunch! And I didn't eat it! So I've got two presents without paying!"

Binny had looked enviously at her golden little brother. His lowered lashes cast an enchanting shadow on his smooth, irrepressible cheek and he looked extremely pleased with himself.

"That was lucky," she said.

"Yes," agreed James.

"Or else what would you have done?"

"I don't know," James had admitted. "I've been looking for money for ages. I did find two pennies on the playground, but Dill said they were his."

So money haunted James as well. Two pennies on the playground. The bourbon creams. Still, he had managed a birthday present for Sunday with very little trouble. Two presents, in fact. Once again, Binny had worried about her own gift of homemade tokens for cups of tea, vacuuming, and putting things away. *(This token when given to Belinda Cornwallis will make her put away a minimum of twenty items! Usable anywhere in the house.)* Her other present, poppy seeds, was all right, but it didn't wrap up into a proper parcel shape, and didn't compare with Clem's present of pearly dangling earrings with little silver shells.

"They only came from the market," Clem had told Binny consolingly, when she found her worrying. "Poppy seeds are perfect, her favorite flower."

Binny had not been much comforted, but it had been the best she could do.

Until now.

Binny walked home in a spending dream. Roses in pots and books of poetry. Dazzling silk scarves and bracelets and perfume. Giant chocolate bars for James and peppermint cremes for Clem. A new hat for Pete whose present one had a hole in the middle. He needed a hat and he had been icy with her ever since she had climbed up the scaffolding. A new hat might warm him up a bit. Also Cinderella, currently living on the cheapest cat food possible, needed sardines, and Max could have a Frisbee for when he came for his vacations, and the chickens, Pecker and Gertie, loved cabbages and . . .

Crash! All four library books fell as Binny walked into a lamppost very hard.

"Sorry, sorry," she murmured to the books and the lamppost, hardly noticing the pain, her mind on her shopping list, her hand guarding the treasure in her pocket. Oh, money! Oh lovely, needed, unlooked-for money! Suddenly she couldn't wait to get home, rush upstairs, spread it out on her bed, and gloat over it, each note, one by one.

Here was the last steep road. Terraced houses rising in steps, flower tubs and cats and trash cans dragged through the front doors from the little gardens at the back because tomorrow was trash day. Binny skirted the last of them and there was her own door with its dolphin shaped knocker, and then she was home.

The rest of the family were also home. James and his friend Dill were upstairs laying out train tracks, a newly revived passion since the discovery of the whistle and the hat. Her mother was in the kitchen with the table covered in newspaper, and a half painted wooden chair on the top. The kitchen chairs were all different shapes, but soon at least, they would be all the same color, apple green with white legs. Binny's mother was painting one a day and this was the last. Tomorrow, when it was dry, nobody would have to sit on the stairs to eat their supper. At present the stairs were occupied by Cinderella, curled into a snow white swirl of cat. The air was filled with the smell of paint from the kitchen, the squawks and squabbles of the boys upstairs, and the sound of Clem's flute in the living room, cascades of notes patterning and repatterning as she worked.

Into this kaleidoscope of family went Binny. Clem nodded to her when she opened the door but did not pause, and Binny retreated back from the room. She wasn't musical like Clem, and she thought flutes might be beautiful to look at, but they sounded like loud mad owls. She headed for the kitchen instead, until her mother called, "Hello Binny! Shoo, till I finish with this paint!"

The problem was where to shoo that was private enough to spread out a pocketful of money. The moment she started up to her bedroom, there was James.

"Hello don't k—" began James, and then, at a splutter from behind, ordered, "Shut up Dill!"

"'Kiss,'" you were going to say!" murmured Dill.

"I wasn't! Don't come upstairs, I was going to say."

"Why not?" Binny asked.

"Because you'll tread on the train lines. Dill'n me have made the Channel Tunnel under your bed."

Binny groaned. One of the many troubles of no bedroom door was no way of keeping out James.

"And," continued James, "you can't go into the bathroom because Dill says it's Paris."

Dill, husky voiced, severe, and seven, said, "Unless you've got a passport."

"What if I want the loo?" demanded Binny.

The boys looked at each other and shook their heads.

"It would still be Paris," explained James, and Dill added, "There aren't any loos in Paris. I went there and there weren't. You have to go up the Eiffel Tower."

"What, everyone?" cried James, delighted. "Everyone in Paris? Even the girls?"

Dill smiled a mouth-turned-down smile, blushing a little and looked sideways at Binny. The family were still getting used to Dill, who had been presented to them without warning as James's new best friend. It seemed to James's family that one moment they had hardly known Dill existed, and the next he had moved in to live with them. Dill went to the same school as James. In class he sat at James's table. After school, and in the vacations, he spent his time at his grandmother's house, a few doors down the street. "So," said James, "he has to be my friend."

"Hmm," said Clem, who had already chased Dill out of her bedroom ("Just lookin'," said Dill), rescued Cinderella the cat from his schoolbag as he was leaving the door ("Just givin' her a ride," Dill explained), and interrupted his exploration of the back of the fridge ("Just wonderin' what to cook").

"I think it's good Dill'n me are friends," said James, and Dill's grandmother agreed. It solved a problem for her that had lasted for years. Seven years, ever since the fateful afternoon when she and Dill had first met and he had looked so quiet and harmless, bundled in a white shawl in a plastic hospital cot. A rare and reckless excitement had swept her senses away that day. "I can help look after him," she had told his grateful parents. "I'll do that."

What she should have added was "*sometimes*." "I'll do that *sometimes*."

Instead of nearly every day, before and after school and all through the school vacations.

Dill's grandmother was exceedingly relieved when James came along, with his home down the road, and his trains, and his useful supply of child-minding big sisters. "Off you go to your friend," she told Dill, the minute he arrived, and off he went, and here he was now.

Binny, with the money burning to be counted in her pocket, the Channel Tunnel under her bed, and Paris in the bathroom, couldn't help sighing. However, there was one closed door in the house, that of Clem's bedroom, and so she called downstairs. "Clem, Clem, can I borrow your room just for one minute?"

Clem, who had not long before moved into the tiniest room in the house on the understanding that no one ever visited her there, yelled back, "No!"

"I need somewhere private," explained Binny, coming halfway down the stairs, and a new voice said, "Ah!"

It was their neighbor, Miss Piper, who had recently moved into the vacation cottage she owned next door. Binny could never see this person in their house without wanting to turn her around, put both her hands in the small of her back, and push her out of the door. That was how Binny felt about Miss Piper and it was all because of the time she had overheard her say to her mother, "If you ever think of selling I would be so grateful if you would give me first refusal."

"*Oh!*" Binny's mother had said.

"Unless, of course, somebody has already asked you the same thing."

"No. No one has. No."

"Thank you, then. Thank you, Polly. I appreciate it. I must go now but that is such a relief."

Binny had glared at Miss Piper's retreating back and demanded, "What's first refusal?"

"Nothing. Well. Nothing that matters. It means that if we ever wanted to sell the house we would ask Miss Piper if she would like to buy it before we asked anyone else."

"I *knew* it was something *awful*."

"Well, to tell the truth Binny, it wouldn't be awful. It would be convenient and helpful and save us quite a lot of money. But of course we're not selling the house to anyone, so you can stop worrying."

Binny hadn't stopped worrying. It was the start of her strange wariness of Miss Piper. Soon after, she had a word to describe that distrust, and although she had never once said it aloud, she knew Miss Piper was aware of it. Aware of it, and slightly amused by it. Sometimes Binny would feel Miss Piper's eyes upon her. Their expression was that of a person doing private sums in her head. It was impossible to tell what she concluded from these calculations. Her voice was always exactly the same. It had a lap, lapping sound, thought Binny, a going-nowhere sound, like the water in the harbor at high tide on a windless day.

However, now Miss Piper was smiling. She stood at the bottom of the stairs and her smile floated up to Binny as she said, "I popped in to see how you were!"

"Me?" asked Binny.

"I was behind you coming up the hill when you walked into that lamppost. Quite a bump. You dropped all your books. I called."

"Did you?"

"You didn't hear. In a dream. In a daze. Dazzled. Bewitched and bedazzled! Were you?"

"No," said Binny, uncomfortable, and untruthful.

Miss Piper raised her eyebrows. Binny fidgeted and was thankful when Clem appeared, still holding her flute.

"Clem!" said Miss Piper. "There you are! Playing your flute again. Do you know, I could hear you away down the street, almost as soon as I came out of the marketplace! Hello, Polly!"

The children's mother looked at Binny and Clem's bothered faces and said tactfully, "Come and see my chairs, Annabelle!" and led Miss Piper away.

"Ignore our growly Binny!" Binny heard her say as the door closed after them, and Miss Piper's reply, "I do see that privacy must be a *great* problem for her and Clem!"

Binny pulled a face at the kitchen door.

"Don't!" said Clem. "Why do you need my room? Is it about Sunday?"

Sunday was their mother's birthday and Binny nodded because it was about that, in a way.

"Oh all right, then. But don't let the boys in. Can people really hear my flute right down the street?"

"No," said Binny. "Take no notice!" She glared again in the direction of the kitchen, but a minute later, safe in Clem's bedroom with her back against the door, she forgot Miss Piper and took out her money.

It was a thick roll of notes. A transforming amount of money. Enough to make nothing impossible anymore. Binny sighed with thankfulness. Her mother's birthday triumphant. Maybe even the next school trip. But birthday presents first! thought Binny. How much were diamonds? Her mother's diamond earrings had not survived the bankruptcy. Imagine producing new ones! *Happy Birthday! You'll never guess what!*

Binny had a money box, lighthouse shaped, usually empty. That night she stuffed it so full that the few small coins already inside hardly had room to rattle. Then she lay in bed and planned her route round the shops the next day. Following this, in bliss, she pictured the birthday morning with an armload of presents. The astonished unwrapping, the exclamations and delight. *Binny, how perfect! My favorites!*

This wonderful feeling lasted all night and was not shattered until morning when Clem asked quite casually, as they washed the breakfast things together, "Do you want to look at the earrings I bought Mum one more time before I wrap them up?"

It was as if Binny had stood on the edge of the sea, thinking, *It's warm! It's gorgeous!* and then been flattened by a wave of absolutely freezing salt water.

Binny floundered and gasped and dropped the mug she was drying to smash on the kitchen floor.

"Binny!" groaned Clem.

"Sorry," Binny said, and after the broken pieces were collected, managed to follow Clem to her room, and agree (rubbing metaphorical salt water from her eyes) that Clem's silver earrings, bought with the hoarded remains of her café earnings (after she had paid for flute lessons, college supplies, birthday cake ingredients, Binny's new hair bobbles, and a comic book for James) didn't look at all like earrings from a market stall, especially now that Clem had found them a proper little box, instead of market bubble wrap.

"They definitely said they were real solid silver," said Clem, inspecting them so anxiously that Binny dismissed completely and forever the thought of diamonds as a birthday surprise.

It was a cold drenching of real life, the very beginning of the problem of being very rich when those around you are very poor. Before Binny had begun to recover from it there came another wave, just as bad.

James said, "You know Dill?"

"Yes."

"Dill said that it was fair for me to give Mum the picture, because it was a picture of me. But it was cheating to give her the Kit Kat because I didn't buy it. Or did he just say that because he wanted us to eat it?"

"Because he wanted you to eat it," said Binny indignantly. "He's a greedy pig and it was brilliant of you to save it for Mum!"

"If I give it to her it makes two presents," explained James earnestly. "Two presents from me. Same as you and Clem."

"Clem?"

"Two earrings."

"Oh yes, I see."

"Fair," said James.

Chapter Four

* * *

Saturday, All Day, Till Night

Binny didn't go shopping that Saturday morning. She couldn't wreck the fairness of James's anxious two presents each. Nor could she upstage those earrings and that worried-over Kit Kat. It would be cheating. Outrageous cheating. Anyway, there was no time to go anywhere because there was the birthday cake to be made.

"Chocolate cake," said Clem, frowning over a recipe book. "We'll start it soon as Mum goes off to work. I hope I've got enough stuff. I'm making a one and a half times the recipe size. Look!"

Binny looked, doing the math aloud as she read. "Three hundred and seventy-five grams of chocolate. Four and a half eggs . . ."

"Oh!" said Clem.

"Make it twice as big," suggested Binny. "It'll be much easier to work out, and we haven't had a proper cake for ages and ages."

Clem, hovering uncertainly between the kitchen and the stairs, said, "I don't think I have enough chocolate. Unless I rush out and get one more bar."

"Good idea!"

"Only, I've just about run out of money, that's the problem. Have you any change, Bin? Would you mind if I raided your money box?"

"NO!"

"Thanks," said Clem, heading up the stairs. "I'll put it back as soon as . . ."

"I meant, No, don't look in my money box!" said Binny, running to push past Clem on the narrow stairs. "Not, No I don't mind! I'll look! You wait down here!"

"All right! All right! How was I to know it was secretly stuffed full of twenty-pound notes! What's the matter now?"

Binny, pale with shock, was staring down the stairs at her.

"Nothing," she croaked.

"Hurry, then," commanded Clem, and to Binny's infinite thankfulness, left her alone to extract the very small amount of cash from her money box that could be reasonably handed over to buy chocolate.

"We'll just manage," said Clem, adding it to her own collection of change. "If I promise not to rob you while you are out, would you scoot to the shop to buy it, Binny?"

"Couldn't you?"

Clem rolled her eyes and dashed out of the door and as soon as she had gone Binny ran for her money box again.

It was the start of a very difficult time.

During the morning, between taking turns to mix the cake, Binny hid the money. First in her school bag, and then, when James wanted to borrow pencils to make a birthday card, in her sock drawer, with the flower seeds and gift tokens. That was all right until Clem said, "Let's get all the presents and see what they look like together in a heap. I know where they are, I'll fetch them!" Binny had to race her upstairs again, rescue her treasure, and push it hastily into her slippers. This lasted until Dill appeared, all eager to construct more railway lines. Binny grabbed the slippers from under her bed and stuffed them up her sweater.

"Are they special slippers?" asked Dill, noticing at once.

"Yes. No. Yes they are."

"No they're not," said James. "They're just your smelly old ordinary slippers."

"Why are you hiding them?" asked Dill.

"I'm not."

"You are," said James, "and you've gone all red!"

Dill murmured something to him.

"What was that?" asked Binny suspiciously.

"He said, 'Let's turn into spies!' That's all."

"Spies!"

"No!" said Clem, overhearing this. "Binny and I are much too busy to put up with spies around here! Railway engineers are bad enough! Spies," she added, looking at Dill, "can go home!"

Dill, who never went home if he could possibly help it, smiled his downward smile, and went back to helping James with the terribly difficult task of building a railway that went upstairs. Binny slipped off and hid the contents of her slippers in her jacket pocket. They stayed there until Clem suddenly groaned, "Icing sugar! I forgot to buy icing sugar! Have you any more change?"

"No," said Binny certainly.

"No money at all?" asked Clem, hunting through her purse. "Check your pockets! Or can I?"

"No!" Binny grabbed her jacket just in time, and very luckily a moment later Clem found a surprise pound coin in the corner of her bag. She hurried out to the shops for a second time while Binny hid the money again. And again, and again, as the morning progressed, and the cake went into the oven, birthday cards arrived in the post, Pecker laid an egg, and the railway engineers, ignoring Clem, became spies in winter hats and dark 3-D movie glasses, skulking at the base of Miss Piper's back fence.

Binny took them the cake bowl out to scrape.

"Evidence!" they hissed to each other, and licked their spoons furtively, with their hats pulled down over their noses. "Could you tell who we were if you didn't know?" asked James, between licks.

"Never," said Binny kindly.

Pete the builder arrived unexpectedly while they were still outside. He brought with him a set of open wooden stairs that he said he'd come by from a friend and was leaving in the garden.

"Why?" asked Binny ungratefully.

"Just a thought," he said, and disappeared indoors with his tape measure.

"Follow!" whispered James to Dill, so they did.

Binny waited until she was quite alone and then climbed swiftly up the apple tree. The summer before she had made a tree house there, consisting of half a surfboard, tied on with washing line. It was so wobbly that no one but Binny ever dared visit it, which made it a perfect hiding place for the money, wrapped in a bread bag and pushed under the board. Binny stayed in the apple tree until a woolly hatted spy popped up at her feet.

"It's only me," said Dill, and Binny groaned, rescued her money before he got any higher and took it back into the house. There she looked around her bedroom.

There was too much stuff. Not just James's train
track and the terrible clutter of everyday belongings,
but half unpacked boxes, a never-played-with dolls'
house, and Max's basket, kept on the floor to remind
herself that he would soon be coming back.

The family were always sorting and stacking and
organizing their belongings. It was difficult because the
house was small, and the never-quite-finished building
work made it even smaller. Only Clem achieved complete tidiness. That was because she owned so little.
Clem's things had a way of vanishing to pay for music
lessons, unless Binny managed to rescue them first. The
dolls' house was a rescue that she sometimes regret-
ted. It had very painful chimneys and the pointyness
of the roof made it impossible to sit on with any sort
of comfort. Binny looked at it crossly, and then had a
good idea.

"James!" she called. "Guess what! I'll give you the
dolls' house! You can use it for a station or a farmhouse
or anything you like!"

"No thank you," said James, arriving at once with
Dill behind him.

"Why not?"

James rolled his eyes at Dill, who murmured as if to
help Binny understand, "He's a boy."

"Makes no difference," said Binny. "Boys need houses
as much as girls. I'll share it with you, then, James.
You have it sometimes and I'll have it sometimes.

I've had it already for ages, so it's your turn now."

"If you give it to me I'll give it to Dill," said James ungratefully.

"All right," said Binny, beginning to tug the dolls' house out of her room. "Here you go Dill! Isn't it lovely?"

Dill shook his head furiously and glared at James.

"He won't be given it," related James.

"Lent, then. I'll lend it to you, Dill!"

Dill breathed hard through his nose.

"He won't be lent it, either!" said James, and shoved the dolls' house out of the way so hard it slid down the first two stairs and jammed, just as the front door opened and a voice called, "Hello!"

"It's Mum! Keep her out of the kitchen!" screeched Binny, and James jumped the dolls' house and clattered down the stairs to spread-eagle himself across the closed kitchen door.

"You can't go in!" he explained. "Clem's made something secret and I'm taking you for a walk while she ices it with Binny. It's all arranged. We're going to the harbor where you might buy me an ice cream. Dill's coming too."

Dill said something very quiet and intense.

"And then coming back after to scrape the icing bowls," translated James.

"Yes I see," said his mother, and went to the harbor very willingly, leaving Clem and Binny to experiment with chocolate and caramel and cream. The wonderful smell of the caramel brought Pete's head poking round the door, where he was so admiring and dropped such large hints that Clem invited him to come and have a slice tomorrow.

"Bring a present, though," Binny ordered.

"Binny!" said Clem, shocked at the idea of demanding a present from the never-paid Pete.

"I will," said Pete. "I know just what she needs. I'll see you tomorrow, then. I'll look forward to that."

Almost as soon as Pete had gone Miss Piper came round.

"Just popping!" she said. "To have a tiny word about James and his friend. Should they be playing with knives, do you think?"

"No they shouldn't!" exclaimed Clem. "What sort of knives?"

"Table knives, I believe. So not a good idea! They were using them to enlarge the gaps in the fence."

"Oh, they were spying!" said Binny without thinking. "Pretend spying, for a game," she added, seeing Miss Piper's smile tighten on her face.

"They won't anymore," said Clem. "I promise. I should have noticed them, but I was so busy with Mum's cake."

"Ah!" said Miss Piper. "Yes I knew there was a birthday coming. And how are you going to keep it hidden until tomorrow?"

"James is having it in his bedroom," said Binny. "It's his reward for taking Mum out while we ice it."

Again she saw the expression on Miss Piper's face, and she remembered her little brother's bedroom, with its potions brewing in jars and its piled up socks, and she hurried to add, "In a cake tin of course. A tin, with a lid. Not bare in his bedroom, getting all hairy!"

Miss Piper said very quickly, although she had not yet been asked, "I never eat cake," and retreated back to her own doorstep. "Don't forget the candles!" she called from her butterfly shaped doormat, and then vanished into her house.

"Candles!" wailed Binny, but Clem had remembered. A pale green one for the middle of the cake. Thirty-nine pink and pale green tea lights, another find from the market, to go round the edge. "Whatever would we do without the market?" asked Clem. "Just think, if we had to buy everything in shops!"

Binny, now infinitely richer than her hardworking sister, felt guilty all over again.

All through that day the money continued to make itself as visible as possible. By evening it had been hidden in Binny's pillowcase, very briefly in the tea light box, her bathrobe pocket, and in an empty cookie tin which was nearly thrown away. That night she took it to bed with her, made the quilt into a tent, and prepared to gloat over it again. She had not yet counted it. Somehow she could not quite bear to do that, it looked such a frightening large amount.

"Night, Binny," said Clem, tiptoeing past her door-way, and Binny's head shot out of the tent in a terrible panic and whacked hard into her headboard. "Ouch!" she moaned. "Oh no! Go away!"

"What have you got there?" asked Clem, not going away at all.

"Nothing, nothing," said Binny, scuffling a lot under her quilt.

"I think you're up to no good!" said Clem. "As usual. Do you want to get up really early and help with a sur-prise birthday breakfast?"

"Oh yes!"

"Okay. If you wake up first come and get me, and if I wake up first I'll come and get you. I thought we'd do hot choc and pancakes, enough for everyone."

"Gorgeous!"

"Night night, then. Shall I put your light out?"

"I might write for a bit."

"Okay, if you must."

Binny's need to write baffled Clem as much as her own flute music did Binny. Clem did not see the charm of smooth paper, or the magic of the ripples and splashes of words as they poured onto the page. Nor did she understand that Binny wrote to untangle her thoughts, as other people doodled, or ran, or listened to music. She just knew that her sister did it. Often. Nearly every day. Understandable things, like the Biography of Max the

Dog, and inexplicable things such as Everything Yellow
I Saw Today, as well as entries in her father's notebook,
in very small writing so as to make it last forever.

That night Binny wrote:

> *I wish Miss Piper hadn't followed me all*
> *the way back from the marketplace.*
>
> *Think about something else! Think about*
> *something else! Think about something else!*
>
> *Okay, Miss Piper and Pete.*
>
> *Miss Piper doesn't like Pete. Especially*
> *his white van with its rusty red patches. She*
> *says it spoils the look of the street. But it's the*
> *best van Pete can manage because he never*
> *gets paid. Mum tries and he says, "PLEASE.*
> *WHEN I'M FINISHED."*
>
> *He was nearly finished until the day that*
> *none of the lights would switch on. Pete*
> *looked at our fuse box (which was full of damp*
> *gray crystals that looked like salt) and he*
> *yelled, "POLLY YOU HAVE NEVER BEEN*
> *EARTHED!"*
>
> *"How do you know?" asked Mum. "I have*
> *been earthed a lot as a matter of fact. I find*
> *having three children very earthing."*
>
> *But Pete said he meant the sort of earthing*
> *that stops the house catching fire when the*
> *live wires touch each other. He didn't like our*
> *wires, he said they were nothing better than*

chewing gum. Before he managed to get rid of
them he got two electric shocks.

"Are you sure he knows what he is doing?"
asked Miss Piper when she heard this news.

"Oh yes," said Mum. "Oh yes, I'm sure he
does. He's put in all-new wiring and a new
fuse box and plugs. We didn't even know we
had a problem!"

We haven't paid Pete yet for all the wires
and things, or for sorting out the windows
so they open and shut. Or for painting the
henhouse or for the little fence he made
around the trash cans so the garden looks
like a garden not a trash patch. He helped
me dig over a place for the poppy seeds as
well, but that was just to be friendly. We are
friendly to him back. When we have baked
potatoes and he is here we put in an extra
one for him. And we make him cups of tea
but he brings his own teabags because he
says ours are wishy-washy. And he likes
toast better than bourbon creams.

Miss Piper has a face she makes when Pete
is around. She smiles and at the same time she
sucks in the corners of her mouth.

I wish I hadn't remembered Miss Piper's face.
I've got all this money.
Pounds and pounds and pounds.

Binny fell asleep with her thoughts all heavy with money. Deep in the night she woke up to realize that her hands were full of twenty-pound notes, recognized the danger of Clem arriving early in the morning and discovering her secret, and staggered out of bed to hide them yet again.

Chapter Five

* * *

Sunday

Binny was woken by Clem shaking her shoulder and then a wonderful day began that started with pancakes and ended with candles and in between included many hugs, as well as exclamations of pleasure, including: "Binny, how perfect! My favorites!"

It was all just as Binny had imagined, only with much less glamorous presents. Straight after breakfast the silver earrings were put on and the poppy seeds were planted and then the first voucher was cashed in for a birthday cup of tea while the Kit Kat was shared with James.

In the afternoon more presents came, the first from Pete.

"Were you on the lookout?" he asked when Binny rushed to the door to meet him. "I hadn't even rung."

"I heard you whistling."

"I wasn't whistling! I was particularly not whistling!"

"*Knock, knock, knocking on Heaven's door!*" said Binny.

"Well, whatever," agreed Pete. "How's your mum?"

"She's having a brilliant time. We gave her loads of presents and she's got two she hasn't unwrapped yet from the old people's home. They gave her a great big card too, with everyone's names on and Clem and me made posh lunch."

"How posh?"

"Soufflé. That's posh! You have to beat up egg whites. Where's your van, Pete?"

"I walked," said Pete, "not wanting . . ." He paused, and glanced over his shoulder in the direction of Miss Piper's windows. Silk flowers filled their sills, and snowy lace curtains draped the panes of glass. Often, it seemed to Binny, there were soft movements behind those curtains, such as Cinderella made when she sat watching from the window at the sparrows in the street.

"She wants to buy our house, did you know?" Binny told Pete. "To make hers bigger for vacation people."

"Half the old cottages are going that way," said Pete. "It's you lot who need more space. It's like trying to work in a monkey cage in there sometimes. Mind you,

you'd have more room if you got rid of the books."

"You can't get rid of books!"

"Why not?"

"You just can't. We used to have a bookshop."

"Isn't the whole idea of a bookshop to get rid of books?"

"No!"

"'Course it is! Common sense!"

"Our bookshop didn't get rid of books. It had thousands! And it had big sofas and little tables with blue bowls of free sweets."

"Very nice," said Pete. "Am I going to be coming in, then, or not?"

"Oh yes, come in!" said Binny, suddenly anxious for Pete not to ask what had happened to the happy place she remembered. The bookshop that had done everything a bookshop should do except get rid of books. "Come in! Did you bring a present?"

Pete had brought a present, and it was a spirit level, secondhand and not wrapped up, and the children's mother could not speak for laughing when she saw it.

"I don't know what's funny," said Pete. "Do you know not a picture in this house is hung straight?"

"Have you ever given anyone a spirit level for their birthday before?" Binny asked.

"I haven't needed to," said Pete, looking down his nose at her. "Everyone I know has got one already.

What's the matter with you?" he added, observing that both Binny and Clem were now dying with laughter too. "If I hadn't got a spirit level and someone gave me one I'd be . . . I'd be . . . thankful!"

The children's mother said she was very thankful indeed and she tried it on several pictures so that they could all watch as the little bubble floated slowly to the point which proved Pete to be right.

"It's all relative," said Clem. "Relative to the spirit level, the pictures are crooked. Relative to the floors and walls and ceilings, they're straight."

Dill, who had arrived uninvited and been very interested in the spirit level, stunned them all by saying huskily, "Nothing can be really straight because the world is round."

"Rubbish!" said Pete.

"It's true!" said James, nodding, while Dill smiled his downward smile, eyes on the ground. "Didn't you know? I thought everyone knew!"

Pete said of course he knew the world was round, and James whispered loudly to Dill, "Pretend you believe him!" and they both curled with silent laughter, hitting each other with pleasure.

"Stop it!" Binny said crossly. "Stop it! It's Mum's birthday! Be good!"

Pete picked up a boy in each hand, opened the kitchen door with his foot, strode into the garden, and deposited them side by side on the henhouse roof.

"You're a natural bouncer!" said the children's mother approvingly.

Pete grinned, began whistling, stopped himself, found his hat, looked at it, put it back in his pocket, and ordered that the spirit level be put somewhere safe. They put it on the mantelpiece, with birthday cards around it, and then James came in to say, as he had been saying at very short intervals all day, "What about birthday cake?" and everyone agreed that it was time.

It was a gorgeous cake, the children's mother said when she saw it, but Pete looked dubious and said the whole thing looked very shaky.

"Shaky?" asked Clem.

"Like it might drop apart," explained Pete, waggling the candle. "See that? Loose! Never pass the fire regs. Whole thing needs reinforcing if you ask me!"

Then he frowned down at Binny in a way that showed he had not forgotten that she had climbed up the scaffolding to check his tiling.

"You don't have to have any," said Binny, rather offended, but he did, and joined in with singing "Happy Birthday" as well.

"It's not quite my daftest present ever," the children's mother said, when he left, not long afterward. "My father once gave me a haggis."

"A *haggis*! What did you do with it?"

"I didn't do anything. I think they are terrible things. My father loved haggis, though, so he ate it.

There's Miss Piper at the door! Open it, James!"

Miss Piper had a birthday present too, properly wrapped in pink tissue paper.

"But," said James, staring as it was finally unwrapped, "even crazier than Pete's!"

It was a doll made out of a clothes peg, the old-fashioned sort of peg with a round knob at the top. That made the head of the doll which was dressed to look, and it did look, exactly like Binny. There she was, gray green eyes, seaweed hair, freckles, jeans, and Clem's old pink and white striped shirt. Under one pipe cleaner arm she carried a miniature notebook. Her other hand was in her pocket.

"Goodness it's wonderful!" exclaimed Binny's mother. "It really is! How clever you are! Binny, look! It's even a real little notebook! It opens!"

Binny was already looking, not at the notebook, but at the hand in the left pocket. *Bang, bang, bang* went her heart.

"It's perfect," said her mother, and Miss Piper smiled and admitted to making very many of these dolls. "For a hobby," she said modestly. "I'd never think of selling them. Oh, I've made them for a long time, ever since I was a girl."

"Were you a girl?" asked James, round eyed, and Dill puffed out his cheeks with unexploded laughter but Miss Piper said calmly, "I was once, a long time ago, a very young, very pretty girl."

There was still something very young about the arrangement of shadows and wrinkles on Miss Piper's face. Her blue eyes and silver curls were almost pretty still. But old-pretty, thought Binny, like a pressed flower instead of a growing one.

Unbidden, Binny's word for Miss Piper came to her just then.

Witch.

Miss Piper's eyes were watching hers.

And she knows I know, thought Binny.

Meanwhile, Binny's mother and Clem were smiling and introducing new friends, Clare from Binny's class at school and Clare's mother Molly. They were comfortably natural, handing over pink wine, a posh magazine, and a box of homemade cherry meringues.

"Rude cakes!" cried James in delight when he saw them, causing Dill's face to turn dark purple, but the mothers placidly arranged them on plates and opened the wine. Even Miss Piper ate one, nibbling primly around the cherry and smiling as her doll was shown and admired.

Witch, witch, witch, thought Binny again, and was glad when she went home.

Later there was a thin slice of moon and an icy spring green evening sky. There was a planet too: Venus, rising as the sun set.

"Now?" asked Clare, looking at her mother, and her mother nodded and produced from behind the sofa a large box of giant sparklers. They lit them in the darkening garden and twirled circles and messages in vanishing bright lines.

"I like rockets best," said Dill, and wonder of wonders, Clare's mother had brought rockets too.

"Thank you for my brilliant day," said the children's mother at bedtime. "I ache from laughing! And the birthday cake, and the presents and the fireworks and the treats. It was perfect."

"Light off?" asked Clem, standing in Binny's bedroom doorway.

"Yes please."

"Finished writing, then?"

"I don't feel like writing tonight."

"Binny?" Clem paused, one hand on the light switch, her silvery charms shining on her arm. "Something wrong?"

"Yes. No. I don't know. Are you going to wear your bracelet always?"

Clem shook her head. "Just sometimes. It would be awful to lose it. Today was lovely, wasn't it? Everybody helped, even Pete."

"Miss Piper didn't."

"I liked her little doll. She said she'd make one of James and me as well."

"Don't let her!"

"Bin! How could I stop her? Why would I want to, anyway?"

"She's a witch," said Binny. "That's why. I've been thinking for quite a long time that she's a witch. I just haven't liked to say it before now."

Clem groaned.

"She's even got a broomstick! I've seen it in her garden. Don't say it's for sweeping leaves because she hasn't got any leaves."

"Binny, do you always have to have an enemy? Aunty Violet? Gareth? Clare? And now Miss Piper! Why?"

"It's the way she's started looking at me."

"Actually," said Clem, unexpectedly, "I did notice her looking at you when she was here this afternoon. Thoughtfully."

"Witchily!"

"Don't be daft!" said Clem, and switched off the light.

Binny lay in the cluttered darkness of her room and thought dreadful, cluttered thoughts.

She looked at me like that because she knows about the money.

The money that I found.

Did she see me?

Nobody saw me.

If I hadn't picked it up, someone else would have.

Or else it would have blown away.

Anyway it wasn't anybody's.

Well, perhaps the bank's.

But

Banks don't have feelings. Banks are just places. Like schools or hospitals or swimming pools.

I didn't steal it.

I definitely didn't.

Did I?

Did I?

Yes.

Chapter Six

✶ ✶ ✶

Monday Morning

The money was the first thing Binny thought of when she woke the next morning, even before she remembered that it was the first day of the mid-term break.

In a few hours her bundle of notes had gone from being a happiness to being a burden. She wished she had never seen it. Hadn't her mother's birthday been perfect as it was? Wouldn't it have been ruined if she'd produced the least glimmer of a diamond? Her Saturday madness and joy was all gone now. She thought, I'm going to give it back, and the thought was absolute bliss.

Although giving it back, Binny realized very quickly, was not going to be half as easy as taking it in the first place. A handful of notes could not just be left at an ATM, unguarded, free to the cold spring wind, or the next grabbing hands. They belonged, Binny supposed, to the bank and that was where they would have to be returned.

Oh.

What would the bank staff say, she wondered, when she arrived at the counter? Might they be so pleased to see their lost property that they would forget to ask where it had spent the weekend? Would they understand that she had never meant to steal it?

I didn't! thought Binny. Me! Steal! I'd never do that! Never!

Then she thought of Miss Piper's murmuring voice. That peg doll Binny with its hand in its pocket, and suddenly she didn't care how they would behave at the bank. It wasn't important. It would be quite fair if they were angry with her. She would agree with them, nodding, *Yes, you are right!* All that mattered anymore was to get it back, quickly, as fast as possible.

Wherever the horrible stuff was.

Where had she last hidden it, the night before her mother's birthday? Bathrobe pocket, thought Binny, and rolled out of bed to reach for it and it wasn't there.

A thin rivulet of coldness, a tiny trickle of alarm, made its way down Binny's spine. She turned her bathrobe inside out and shook out the sleeves.

No money.

Of course! Of course! She had taken it out of the pocket again when she had noticed the bulge it made. It was in the empty cookie tin on the bookshelf.

No it wasn't, no it wasn't, no it wasn't.

Nor was it in her musical box. Had it ever been in the money box? It had been in the apple tree, her slippers, a bread bag, and her socks. Where else had it been? Binny was swept by a wash of horrible panic.

Somewhere in this room was a bundle of twenty-pound notes.

Definitely in this room; she remembered taking them to bed.

But they were not in her bed, nor in the pillowcase. They were not in her jeans pocket, or any of the drawers in the chest of drawers. Not in Max's basket nor in her pencil case. Not transformed into very expensive book-markers to mark a place in *The Railway Children*, *A Little Princess*, or any of the other books from the half unpacked box. Binny knew this for certain because she took the books out one by one and shook them. It was not beneath her socks in her shoe box of socks, or amongst the washing in the washing basket on the landing, or under her mattress.

It was not under her bed, not in her wardrobe, or on top of it.

Not amongst the trash in her trash can, or the kitchen trash, the bathroom trash, or the big trash can in the garden. Probably not in the apple tree either, definitely

not, it was madness to look, but, still in her pajamas, Binny climbed up and looked.

Since she was passing, she looked in the henhouse too, but it wasn't there.

Binny returned inside, rather muddy.

The money was not in the bag of dog biscuits that she kept on her bedroom windowsill. It was not in James's school bag, nor flattened under the train track. Not in the living room. Not folded into the sofa bed where her mother slept so that lucky Clem and James and Binny could have a bedroom each. Not down the sides of either the pink chair or the rocking chair. Not in, or under, the birthday cake tin.

Not amongst the books on her bedroom bookshelf, or lurking with her old teddy bears in the box where they had been hibernating for the last three years or so. Not, she concluded after a swift ransacking, keeping nice and warm in the cupboard, amongst the folded towels.

Not in any other place that she could think to search.

The money was lost.

None of the family noticed Binny's panic. Her mother, beset by builders' bills, had hurried to work before six that morning, long before anyone else was awake, leaving Clem in charge. James was in the living room, dreamily eating cereal. He was half watching TV, half waiting at the window for Dill to appear. Clem was invisible, shut in her bedroom, playing her flute. Something was wrong in there too: the owl notes were not as clear as usual, they repeated over and over, windy and distorted and tormenting. After Binny had started to notice them she couldn't stop hearing them. They made it impossible to think and she paused her frantic searching to beat her fists on Clem's door and cry, "It's awful, Clem! Stop it!"

"I know, I know," she heard Clem call. "I can't stop it."

Binny returned to her room and began grabbing and shaking things. She did this for a long time, whimpering a bit. Then James erupted in her doorway, with Dill behind him, and demanded indignantly, "*What* have you done to our railway?"

Binny's room looked burgled. Its doors and drawers gaped open. Books lay in heaps. Clothes were piled in landslides. The railway system was engulfed. There was no longer a route to Paris, or anywhere else. There was nowhere that a foot could safely tread. All but the highest landmarks had disappeared.

"Go away," said Binny, but James and Dill only crowded closer.

"I lost something," said Binny.

The devastation overflowed like a wave across the landing, lapped into James's room, mingled with the contents of the cupboard, and poured down the stairs.

Dill, thoughtfully studying the toes of his red socks, spoke a few hushed words to James.

"He said, 'What did she lose?'" said James. "What

did you lose, Binny? Me and Dill will help you look."

Binny shook her head.

"We want to," said James, and Dill, who liked nothing more than ransacking through other people's stuff, nodded in agreement. After that, for what seemed like hours and hours to Binny, the two of them hounded her with discoveries. "*Is it this? Is it this? Is it this?*" they demanded, holding up random items, papers, socks, spare dog collars, books, small trodden-on treasures, and a hundred other things until Binny fled the house to sit hunched on the kitchen doorstep. She remained there until the sky began splattering a thin rain and she realized that she was still in her pajamas. Very slowly she returned to the house and set off up the stairs. James spotted her at once and said brightly, "We're still looking! Is it this?"

He waved a broken pen that had once written with gold ink.

"That's not treasure," criticized Dill. He was holding Binny's jacket. "Yuk, crumbs," he said critically, feeling in a pocket, and Binny leaped to grab.

But the jacket pockets were empty of skulking twenty-pound notes.

The dreadful mad owl noises from Clem's flute had stopped, and while Binny had been searching her jacket pockets, her sister's door had opened. Binny looked up to see Clem gazing down the stairs. Clem was a tidy person and Binny, mud covered and ankle deep in a sea of clutter, waited for her cries of horror. They did not come. Clem stepped through the turmoil as if she didn't see it, her flute case in one hand, her bag in the other.

"Binny, I'm going out," she said as she passed. "I've got to. I won't be long. Look after the boys."

"Me?" asked Binny, but Clem was already gone.

Dill looked questioningly at James.

"Clem was the grown-up," James explained. "Now Binny's the grown-up."

Binny slumped down onto the stairs and dropped her head into her arms. She didn't want to be the grown-up. She wanted someone to come and look after her, put everything away, and then wind back time so that she could walk safely past the ATM without a glance in its direction.

"Clem's supposed to be the grown-up," James continued to Dill. "The boss. When Mum isn't here, it's Clem."

Dill nodded, looked at Binny, hopeless as a grown-up, nothing like a boss, and said, "It's rubbish looking for her treasure. Let's go and bury our own!"

"Where?" asked James. "Outside? In the garden?"

Dill shook his head.

"In your grandma's garden?" asked James, hopefully. He had never yet been invited to Dill's grandma's house.

Dill shook his head again. "On the beach," he said.

"*Now? On the beach?*"

James, aged six, was allowed to go to the baker's on the corner by himself. He was allowed to walk to school with Dill and Dill's grandma. He was allowed to go to Gareth's house on one side, when Gareth's family were visiting, and once, when his elastic band powered airplane had flown over the garden fence, he had been allowed to go to Miss Piper's and ask for it back. Sometimes he was planted in the library when storytelling was going on. Binny had once abandoned him on the pier.

But he had never been to the beach alone. Never. Had Dill?

"I'm seven," Dill reminded him.

It was the way he said it. Like a person might say, "I have superpowers." James had been quite happy being six until he met Dill. And anyway, who said six couldn't go to the beach?

Dill looked at James, hands in pockets, as if waiting for him to admit the uselessness of six.

James pondered.

"The beach, but not swimming," he said at last, because although he had a wetsuit, pink and lime green, a lucky find from a trash can, these days it was only used in the warmth of the bath.

"Digging," said Dill.

"Digging up treasure?"

"Bury it first," said Dill. "Bury it. Make a map. Dig it up later."

"Wow!" said James, overcome at the magnificence

of this plan. "Yes! Have you got any treasure?"

"Mmm." Dill smiled his downward smile. "At Gran's."

"We've got a spade," said James excitedly. "Spade. Paper. Pencil. We've got everything! Bin! Did you hear? You're the grown-up!" He prodded her hunched shoulders to make sure she was still awake. "Dill and me are going treasure burying. Okay?"

Binny heard all this, about the treasure and the map, and how she was now the grown-up. It made no sense to her. All she could think of was the vanished money. It could not be more than a dozen steps away, because the house was so small nowhere was farther away than that. She closed her eyes and tried to detect it by the power of divination. When this didn't work she tried wishing she was dead, as she often did when life became inconvenient.

Meanwhile, the house became very quiet.

Chapter Seven

***

Monday Afternoon, Part One

Clem was the first of the family to return home. She was still slightly dazed from the worry that had sent her out, but, temporarily at least, she was back in the everyday world again. As soon as she closed the front door behind her she noticed the silence. Crossing the hall and the kitchen she peered into the garden.

No James and no Dill. Clem began to feel uneasy. Dill spent school vacations with his grandmother who lived a few doors down the street. Dill's grandmother was a woman who believed in early independence. This meant encouraging Dill to visit his friends as often as possible for as long as possible, consuming as many meals as necessary along the way. Nor did

Dill's grandmother encourage him to bring friends back. It was very unlikely that the boys had gone to her house, thought Clem, remembering how often James's "Let's go to yours now" had been answered with a husky "Let's not."

Then Clem came to the foot of the stairs and saw the wreckage that had cascaded down from Binny's room, and started panicking.

"James! Dill! Binny!" she shouted, and after a moment heard a startled, "What?"

Binny's face peered down at her through the banisters.

"What's happened?" demanded Clem. "Why is there stuff all over the stairs? Where are the boys?"

Binny looked around, blinking. After a moment or two she said rather blankly, "They must have gone."

"Gone where? Binny, wake up! Where are they? You must know!"

Binny, coming slowly back to the world, found she did know. Maps, and digging and burying treasure. A spade and paper and a pencil.

The beach.

"The beach!" exploded Clem. "Those two! On their own! Do you mean on their own?"

Binny nodded unhappily.

Then Clem, the serene, the unselfish one, exploded.

"I was hardly gone any time! Half an hour! Couldn't you have taken care of them for half an hour!"

"I . . . ," began Binny.

"Aren't you old enough! Nearly thirteen!"

"I . . ."

"It isn't fair! Ever since Dad died, all these years, I've had to be grown-up! Mum and me looking after you and James!"

"I . . ."

"How can I do anything? How can I go to university? How can I go anywhere while you are so . . . so . . . helpless!"

"Me?"

"*Look* at you! Just sitting there! Doing *nothing*."

Clem was not doing nothing. All the time she had been shouting she had also been dragging on her old coat, checking the battery of her mobile phone, and rushing for the door.

"Clem! Where are you going!" shouted Binny. "Clem, wait!" And then she began hurrying herself, an old sweater over her pajama top, jeans over the bottoms, bare feet in her school shoes, racing after Clem, calling, "Wait! Wait! Wait!" slipping and stumbling on the wet cobbles as she ran.

She left the door of the house wide open behind her, and that was the way Miss Piper found it.

By the time Binny managed to catch up with Clem they had reached the almost empty beach. With its closed up beach huts and the gray sea spitting and churning in the rock pools it looked very unwelcoming.

"There's no one here," said Binny, although that was not quite true. There were some head-down-against-the-wind grim walkers, two entirely-dressed-in-black surfers, a middle-aged couple with a small dog and a huge kite, but no little boys.

"Are you sure they said they were coming here?" demanded Clem.

"I think so."

"Bin?"

"Yes, yes they did. What had we better do?"

The difficulty was that the beach was not an isolated place. It looked it from above, but really it was one of a long chain of beaches and little coves that looped round headland after headland, all along that stretch of the Cornish coast.

"You go right and I'll go left!" ordered Clem. "Okay?"

It wasn't okay at all, thought Binny. What was she to do if she found the boys? She hadn't her phone with her; she wouldn't be able to stop Clem from carrying on her own search to the left.

And what was she to do if she didn't find them? At what point would she turn back? And, hardest of all, how could she ask these questions without making Clem say "helpless" once again?

There were other things that she would have liked to talk to Clem about as well. The lost money question.

Could Clem possibly have picked up and tidied away a pile of twenty-pound notes without noticing? Clem was such a swift and ruthless tidier that she could almost believe it might have happened.

Binny had turned right and begun her trek along the sands as soon as Clem had ordered it, but now she paused to look back. Her sister was already far away, stomping along with her fists in her pockets, terribly bothered about James being alone on the beach. *Let James be safe,* willed Binny, as she watched her. *Let them both be safe,* and she looked anxiously toward the sea. Pete had told them about the fierce currents that ran round their part of the coast, riptides, he called them, strongest in spring and autumn. James had been intrigued, and mentioned his precious pink and lime green wetsuit . . .

At this thought, Binny detoured to climb a sandbank and peer out to sea, but except for the two insane surfboarders it was reassuringly empty, a restless tarnished pewter ocean, uninvitingly gray.

Binny need not have worried.

Half an hour earlier, James and Dill, arriving at the beach very breathless after a nerve-racking detour to collect Dill's treasure, had hardly bothered to glance at the sea.

"Let's see your treasure properly!" James had said to Dill.

"All right," Dill had agreed, and had obligingly pulled out the object that he had sneaked into his gran's house to retrieve while James jiggled impatiently on the doorstep.

"A tin?" asked James.

"The treasure's all wrapped up inside," said Dill. "That's where I keep it. Gran doesn't know. No one does. Gran doesn't know I've got the tin either. It's a coffee tin. I found it in her sideboard."

"What's a sideboard?"

"Her smelly cupboard. It's got her booze bottles in it, and Dead Granddad's ashtrays, and all the photos she doesn't like looking at, and this tin.

James took the tin and looked at it more respectfully. It was red and gold, with pictures on the sides.

"Bare ladies!" said James, turning it as he inspected them. "Four! Four bare ladies, Dill!"

Dill blushed, but did not deny it. He loved the bare lady tin. His only regret was that the ladies had such long and waving hair.

"It's nearly really rude!" said James. "You can easily tell they're not wearing anything *anywhere*!"

Dill smirked and took the tin back for another look himself. He had not expected such appreciation from someone as young as James. One day, he thought, he might show him the calendar he had discovered in Dead Granddad's old shed. Meanwhile, however, there was treasure to be buried.

"Where?" he murmured, scrutinizing the beach. "Here? Near the steps?"

"There's people," said James critically.

"Not looking at us, though," said Dill.

"They might," said James, "specially when we start digging. They might see that we're digging and come over and stare."

Dill fidgeted uneasily at this suggestion. He didn't like being stared at. His grandmother was a great starer. She would come into a room where he was doing something privately and peacefully, and stand quite still and stare. Then she would start shouting. Dill particularly hated the thunderous silence of the pause between the stare and the shouting. One such silence had happened only that morning when he and his supersoaker had flooded the freezer in an attempt to make snow.

"It's no good trying to do something private if there's people about," said James.

Dill nodded, thinking of his lost supersoaker.

"We'll do it properly," said James. "Follow me!" And he led the way along the beach, so that Dill had to hurry after him, more than a bit indignant, since he was the one who was seven, not James, and he was the one with the treasure to bury and it had been his idea in the first place.

"Stop, stop!" he called at intervals, but every time they paused it was the same. There was always some person lurking in the distance who might potentially stare. It took a long time to find a place with no people at all, but at last they did, and then it was Dill's turn to be the bossy one. James was allowed one last look at the bare ladies and then ordered to close his eyes and not look while Dill very secretly dug.

"What we're doing is a deathly secret," he told James. "Deathly! Okay?"

"Deafly?"

"Yes."

"Okay," said James, wondering what a deafly secret was and secretly feeling his ears. Might it stop them working? "Deafly," he agreed, absolutely determined not to ask. "When can I look?"

"When I say."

This was very chilly and boring for James, and not at all how he had expected treasure burying to be.

"Hurry!" he commanded, many times, but each time, Dill, pacing and counting and squinting at rocks, would growl, "Shush! This is important!"

Even after the measuring and digging were finished and James was allowed to uncover his eyes there was still the map to be drawn. Dill did this leaning over a driftwood plank with the paper hidden in his arms. He took so long that James went off with the spade and buried, with equal secrecy, a handful of white shells, his mother's birthday cake candle, and a very recent find, pocketed only that day from the sands.

After this they went home, keeping close under the shadow of the cliffs where the wind seemed a little less cold. If they had looked out toward the sea they would have seen Binny, head down, eyes screwed half shut against the sandy wind. However, they did not look. They were much too engrossed in being mysterious with each other.

"What did you bury for treasure?" asked Dill.

"Ha!" said James. "What did you?"

"You saw the tin. The bare lady tin."

"I didn't see what was in it."

"You didn't do another thing too," said Dill smugly. "You didn't make a map."

"I can remember," said James. "Easily."

"Easily!" scoffed Dill, pirouetting like a scrawny sand imp. "Easily!"

James picked up a tangle of rotting bladderwrack, dead crab, and someone's faded underwear, rugby tackled Dill, and shoved it under his superhero vest. They writhed on the damp sand, kicking and whacking, until James sat up with his hair full of ancient, stinking crab fragments and said, "Anyway, I left a sign."

"What sort of sign?" asked Dill, inspecting the underwear, screwing them into a ball, and then hurling them at James's head.

"A seagull's feather."

Dill's eyes slid sideways and his mouth turned down at the corners.

"What?" demanded James, who knew a sinister smile when he saw one.

"A feather!" said Dill.

"So?"

"It'll blow away. You should have made a map."

James jabbed crossly at the sand with the spade, burying the underwear. He knew it would blow away. He knew he should have made a map.

"Anyway," said Dill, who didn't like anyone except himself having secrets, "what was it you buried?"

"Shells and stuff," said James evasively.

"What sort of stuff?"

Although James had not actually seen Dill accidentally drop anything on the beach, he did not want to answer that question. To avoid it he set off very quickly in the direction of home, walking so rapidly that it was almost a trot. Dill hurried after him, as speedily as he could while conducting an urgent searching of his pockets.

"Slow down!" he commanded, but James only trotted faster, until Dill stopped completely, knelt down, and emptied out his pockets on the sand. James watched apprehensively, walking backward.

"Where's it gone?" demanded Dill.

"What?" asked James, but he couldn't help his eyes sparkling, and Dill looked up and understood.

Then Dill gave such a dreadful shriek that James was truly frightened. He dropped the spade and sprinted. He ran for what seemed miles and miles. Over the wet beach, straight through shallow tide pools, dodging barnacled rocks, dogs, and kite flyers, and at last across the final soft slope of sand to the steps. Then up the steps and galloping past the harbor.

And all the while he ran, Dill pounded after him, and he called to James in a hoarse nightmare screech, "I'll kill you! I'll kill you! I'll kill you!"

However Binny, far away, knew nothing of all this as she continued her lonely plod across the empty sands.

The children's mother was having a very worrying time. She had been in the middle of her shift at the old people's home when she was called to the telephone.

"Polly dear, are you sitting down?" asked Miss Piper, and her always placid voice was so extremely calm that the children's mother was instantly alarmed.

"Sitting down? Sitting down?" she repeated. "Why should I sit down? What's happened? Is it the children? I can't sit down; I'd get the sack! For goodness' sake, just tell me?"

"I am so sorry, Polly!" said Miss Piper. "I'm afraid it's the house . . ."

"Not the roof *again*!" interrupted the children's mother, sounding quite desperate.

"The door is standing wide open," said Miss Piper. "I've been in and called. There seems to be no one at home."

"No one at home?"

"And I'm afraid it looks very much like . . . do sit down for a moment . . . you've been burgled!"

"Burgled?"

"Yes."

"*Burgled?*"

"Unfortunately yes."

"But what could they possibly *take*?" demanded the children's mother. "And *where* are the children?"

"They do seem to be away," admitted Miss Piper, "but I'm sure you need not worry about that. Clem is almost grown-up and sensible, after all, and Binny is nearly thirteen . . ."

"Yes, but James!" interrupted their mother wildly. James was not remotely grown-up or sensible. His mother pictured his smooth bright head and wicked dark eyelashes, golden tipped, enchanting, the veils for so many smoldering plots, and lost her head completely.

"I'm coming home! I'm coming home now!" she cried, and ten minutes later, by leaving half the residents unserved, forgetting her bag and jacket, and running all the way, she was home.

It was true.

There was Miss Piper on the doorstep and the front door wide open, exactly as described.

"There was no need for quite such a rush!" said Miss Piper.

But the children's mother took no notice and raced through the house, flinging open doors and calling, "James! Binny! Clem! Where are they? Where are they? Oh, where is James? Kidnapped?"

"I'm sure not kidnapped," said Miss Piper. "Why would anyone do that? I expect they are quite safe. They must have gone out, and then, I suppose, whoever it was who turned the place upside down, arrived. I looked, but there are no marks on the front door to show it's been forced. Who has a key?"

"A key? A key?"

"I suppose Clem and Binny have keys? You didn't give the builders a key, did you Polly?"

"Only Pete, for his finishing off. He comes when he has a spare hour or two. He finds so many things to do."

"I'm sure he does!"

The children's mother turned very quickly and looked at Miss Piper.

"All builders find things to do," said Miss Piper, smiling. "The question is, do they need doing? Well, I suppose you have to trust him to some extent but . . ."

She was interrupted just then by a dreadful fishy smell, accompanied by a wet, grimy, sandy, seaweedy, dead-crabby sight.

"Hello, don't kiss me!" said James.

James was in no danger of being kissed. Quite the opposite, and his eyelashes couldn't save him. He was grabbed, de-sneakered, and hauled out of his filthy jacket, hustled into the garden to have sand slapped off his unspeakable jeans, dumped on a newspaper in the kitchen and dared to step off it while dead crab was picked from out of his hair, and all the while indignantly questioned.

"*What has* been happening? *Where* have you been? *How* did you get in this state?"

"It's only sand," said James.

"Soaked! Look at you!"

"There's always wet bits on the beach."

"On the *beach*?"

"I had to run."

"What do you mean, you had to run? Where are the girls?"

"Binny was here," said James. "Sitting on the stairs. Clem went out."

His mother left him to dash to the stairs, as if somehow she might have overlooked Binny sitting there. Miss Piper murmured in very quiet not-for-James-to-listen-to capital letters, "P-O-L-I-C-E?"

"Police?" asked James, who was inconveniently good at the spelling-words-out trick. "Why, what have you done?"

But James's mother was calmer now, and thinking a little more logically. Instead of calling the police, she called Clem on her mobile. After this she became very much less worried and very much more angry, and she explained to Miss Piper that apparently the house had been ransacked by Binny, not burglars, and that it was the girls who had left the door open, rushing out to hunt for James.

"And James was on the beach alone?" asked Miss Piper.

"With Dill," said James sulkily.

"Dill? Well where is Dill now?" demanded his mother.

"At his gran's never speaking to me again."

"Are you sure? Are you sure he's safe home?"

"He went in the door. I heard his gran yelling," said James, fidgeting crossly on his newspaper. "Like you are now, only not so loud."

"I'm not yelling at all!" said his mother, suddenly and quietly dignified. "I'm just very angry. You know quite well you are not allowed on the beach."

"I've been there loads of times," said James.

"Not without someone older than you."

"I had Dill! He's seven! That's older than me. And anyway, Binny let me."

"Don't you go blaming other people as if you hadn't a brain of your own!" retorted his mother. "Do you know how worried poor Miss Piper and I have been?"

"I was about to call the police," said Miss Piper.

"That would have been good," said James, perking up at the thought. "You still could! And tell them Dill put dead crab in my hair."

"You are a very silly little boy and you are lucky to be home safe," snapped his mother. "Now stop arguing, take off those dreadful jeans, there, where you're standing . . . don't move from that spot . . . and then upstairs and get into the shower. I must ring Clem again, and see if she's met Binny. Oh, what an awful day!"

Chapter Eight

✳ ✳ ✳

Monday Afternoon, Part Two

Far away on the sands, utterly hopeless, cold and forlorn, Binny was also thinking, *What an awful day.* James was lost, and it was her fault. The money was lost, and that was her fault too. She realized now that she had stolen it and the knowledge was like a great secret burden that she must drag wherever she went. Neither her mother nor Clem could ever be told. Binny knew too well what would happen once they knew. Somehow, however difficult, however many hours of bathing old ladies and washing dishes in the café it would involve to earn the money, they would save it up and give it back. Since the bankruptcy of the family when Binny's father died, neither her mother nor Clem could bear the thought of owing money.

Dad! thought Binny, and surprised herself at how angry she felt that he was not here to help. Not that he was much good at looking after money anyway, but at least he could have listened. It would have been less lonely. Had he been lonely when he realized, and kept secret, that knowledge that the bookshop money was all gone?

How could he not have been, thought Binny, and forgave him.

The main beach where she and Clem had started their search for the boys was behind her now. She had rounded a promontory and had crossed another, the one with the caravan site above. Now she was plodding along a third beach, smaller and rockier. No James and Dill here, either. If they were not safe it was her fault, the direct result of her madness in the marketplace. She wailed aloud, "What can I doooo?" and the herring gulls, hunched against the wind at the waves' edge, glanced at her in yellow eyed disgust.

I wish I was a gull, thought Binny enviously, with nothing to lose but feathers.

Ahead of her now, was a point where the cliffs reached right out to the waves. Here the sea broke and swirled round the tumbled rocks at their base and there was no more sand. Binny had never been so far away from the town before. She looked uneasily up at the granite boulders that blocked the way. Possibly, before the tide rose so high, the boys had scrambled round that headland, but somehow she did not think so. No footprints showed on the hard wet sand.

All the same, Binny did not turn back. Instead she found a low boulder and hunched down on it. There was nothing to hear but the wild sound of the waves, nothing to see but a tear-blurry wash of rock and sand, and nothing to feel but a sort of cold, numb weariness.

For a long time she stayed that way.

The tide crawled higher, dislodging the gulls. They screamed as they rose and swirled above the waves, and at the same moment Binny was knocked sideways by a great force.

Something was upon her, bounding and alive. Thick silky fur was warm against her face.

"Max!" cried Binny.

Right on cue, the sun escaped the last rags of cloud and flung gilt reflections across the sea. The gulls glittered in the new brightness and the waves broke on the granite in fountains of white light.

"Max!" murmured Binny, with her arms around him. "Max."

The wind, sharp as a silver knife now, was cutting the clouds into streamers and banners. Max and Binny hugged and hugged each other, and Binny asked aloud, "But how did you get here?"

"How do you think?" demanded a voice, and Binny looked up.

There, silhouetted against the bannered sky, stood

Gareth, dreadful hair, hideous glasses, hands in pockets, too wide jeans sagging over gruesome sneakers, best of enemies, most loyal of friends.

He gazed down at Binny with twitching lips, as if absolutely determined not to grin.

"Gareth!" exclaimed Binny, jumping up and hugging him. "Oh Gareth, why didn't you say you were coming?"

"Surprise," said Gareth, disentangling himself very promptly. "Don't get too happy. We're just here till Friday."

"You and your dad and your stepmother?"

"Yes, it was her idea. Just last night. And Dad said okay (he wouldn't have if I'd suggested it) and he and I drove down this morning with Max, we picked him up from Mum's house, and *she's* coming later . . ."

"Your mum?"

"No, no!"

"Your stepmother?"

"Yes, her. She might be here now. I don't know. Anyway, when I arrived I went straight round to yours next door and there was your mum going bonkers. And so was Clem."

"Did you see James?"

"James was the only one behaving normally. He came charging downstairs out of the bathroom when he heard me. That old woman with the silly voice from the house on the other side of you was there too. Going on about burglars."

"Did Miss Piper have burglars?"

"No. 'Course not. She thought you had! It's all right, you haven't. Your house just looks like they've been."

"That was me. Are they furious?"

"Not as bad as my parents would have been if I'd wrecked our place like that. Your mum was more worried about you. She kept saying you'd never learned to swim properly and what about the lifeboat. She was getting really bothered. Clem was trying to calm her down and I said I'd take Max and go and look for you. I was to text her if I found you. I've already done it; I saw you from way back."

"Thank you."

"I guessed you'd done something mad . . . You have, haven't you?"

Binny nodded, her face buried in Max's fur.

"Go on, then! What?"

"Promise you'll never tell?"

"Okay. If you like."

"I stole a lot of money from a bank."

Gareth whistled.

"It was just there, at the ATM outside and I took it. I think Miss Piper saw me."

"Crikey, Bin!"

"And it's even worse than that because I've lost it. I can't find it anywhere."

"How much money?"

"It was a pile of twenty-pound notes. I don't know how many. I didn't count them."

"*What?*"

"I didn't dare."

"You really are seriously weird sometimes," said Gareth sternly. "It can't be lost; it'll be somewhere in all that mess at your house. What'll you do when you find it, anyway?"

"Give it back of course. That's all I want to do now. Give it back quick, before Miss Piper tells. I've looked everywhere, Gareth. I promise I have."

"Still," said Gareth, trying to be reasonable, "there's no need for such a terrible fuss. ATMs don't give out thousands. The most it'll have been is a hundred or two. Even if it is lost, and I don't see how it can be, it wouldn't take forever to pay that much back. You should tell your mum. She'd help."

"I don't think you understand about our sort of money, Gareth," said Binny, looking up at him. "It's not the same as your sort. It's completely different. Your sort is heaps. Our sort is just enough, with none left over."

Gareth shuffled a bit awkwardly. He was an expensive only child with a huge allowance. It was true that he constantly forgot that Binny survived on free school lunches and the odd, rare pound coin. It was hard for him to imagine such an existence, and he mumbled, "Sorry," not wanting to think about it, and then suddenly had an idea.

"Max is good at finding stuff! Hide a ball, and he finds it, every time. Same with lots of things! Toys, hats . . . anything!"

Hope shone across Binny's face and then faded.

"I know," she said. "But he has to know what he's looking for, doesn't he? You have to show him the thing you want him to find first, and then hide it."

"So?"

"So it wouldn't work with something already lost."

Gareth explained patiently that Max found things by smell, and that probably one twenty-pound note smelled pretty much like another.

"Yes but . . ."

"You haven't stolen all the twenty-pound notes in the country," pointed out Gareth. "Just a few of them. There are plenty left for Max to practice with. I've got a couple myself."

"Oh!" exclaimed Binny, when she understood what Gareth was suggesting. "Oh, what a brilliant idea! Oh, thank goodness you and Max are here! Come on! Let's get back! When can we do it?"

"If you want to keep it secret we'll have to wait until people are out of the way," said Gareth, as they both began to walk back along the beach. "So not tonight. Anyway, we're going out to supper as soon as she's arrived . . ."

She, was Gareth's way of referring to his recently acquired stepmother. It was strangely infectious.

"She's nice, you shouldn't talk about her like that," said Binny.

"Huh!" said Gareth.

"I thought you liked her now."

"I suppose she's all right. She's still allergic to dogs, though. That's why she's driving down in her car separately, so as not to be with poor Max."

"She can't help being allergic."

"She never seems to try! Anyway, when she gets here we're going to a pub to save anyone cooking. Do you want to come with us? Dad said to ask you."

Meals out were a great treat, far beyond the Cornwallis family budget, and Binny liked Gareth's furious tempered father and his gentle wicked stepmother, but all the same, she hesitated.

"Are you going to be awful to her all the time?"

"No. Of course not."

"You were when I went out with you once before."

"I've almost got used to her. She's not really any worse than Dad. He was dead annoying driving down. He talked all the way about babies."

"Babies? Gosh!"

"He asked me if I liked them! What kind of a question is that? I said I'd never met one. Where would I meet a baby!"

"Perhaps they are wondering about having one," Binny suggested, "and he wanted to know what you thought."

"Well, he knows now because I told him," said Gareth.

With her new hope of Max finding the lost money, Binny could think of other things, and she could see that this sudden new mention of babies was worrying her friend, so she asked, "What did you say?"

"I made a list of problems," said Gareth smugly.

"Go on, then!" prompted Binny.

"I said: One. This planet is very overpopulated and you've already got me . . . What's so funny?"

"Nothing. Two?"

"Two. You are both too old."

"Are they?"

"Geriatric. Three. I guessed you'd ask me this one day so I googled the cost of child-rearing from zero to university and it's about two hundred thousand pounds not counting driving lessons. That would buy more than three thousand acres of Amazon rain forest which would be much more sensible."

"Yes it would," said Binny, impressed.

"Four. She's allergic to dogs. How do you know she's not allergic to babies? Five. Who would look after it when you're both playing golf?"

A sudden mood of airy hilarity swept over Binny, which Gareth ignored.

"Six. I'm not sitting in the back of the car with it. That was all I could think of, but he hadn't considered a single one of those things himself. He admitted it."

"Was he cross?" asked Binny, who knew from experience that Gareth's father could become very cross indeed.

"No. He said I'd been helpful."

"Did you say, 'And what if it was twins?'"

"No, but that's brilliant! I will do," said Gareth. "There's worse than twins, too! What do they call it when there's three?"

"Triplets. And quads is four."

"Fantastic. Thanks Bin! Quads!"

"Although," said Binny, "if they had quads, or triplets, or twins, or even one single ordinary quite small baby, it would mean that they would be totally distracted from bothering about you. So you could do just about what you liked forever and ever . . ."

Gareth gave Binny a very startled look.

". . . unless you like being an only child . . . Do you?"

"Me?"

"Fussed over . . . I wouldn't. You don't!"

"Of course I don't!"

"How old is she?"

"Thirty-two, I mean, *thirty-two*! Ancient!"

"My mum's forty. Poor old Mum. How'll she pay nine thousand acres of rain forest for Clem and James and me?"

"Hmm," said Gareth.

"It doesn't matter about sitting with it in the back-scat of the car because you've got two cars so you wouldn't have to. I don't know about being allergic to it, or the world being overpopulated. Maybe some very old person will die and make space."

"You can shut up now Binny, if you like," said Gareth.

"You could offer to look after it while they play golf! That would solve that problem."

The wet beach was dazzling with reflected light, the wind fizzed with salt, and whales and possibilities. Max raced the gulls and barked at the waves. Gareth, feeling virtuous, collected plastic litter from the tide-line. Binny forgot that she had ever been alone, and was happy.

"Belinda Cornwallis, you have some explaining to do!" said Binny's mother when Binny finally appeared, with Max and Gareth behind her. "Hello Gareth, thank you for texting. Binny, whatever were you thinking of, to turn the house upside down like this?"

"I was just looking for something," said Binny, her exhilaration fading fast at the look on her mother's face.

"Well, I hope you found it!" said her mother crossly. "Miss Piper thought we'd been burgled, and I'm not surprised. You'd better apologize to her for worrying her so much."

"Now?" asked Binny, horrified. "I can't! I really can't! I'm going to supper in a pub with Gareth and his dad and her."

"You are going nowhere," said her mother calmly, "until every single thing you pulled out is put tidily away."

"Oh Mum!" said Binny.

"Oh Binny!" said her mother. "Get on with it!"

It took ages and ages. Gareth and his father and stepmother waited hungrily for nearly two hours, and then went off without her, promising that the next day (should the tidying be finished by then) they would go again and this time take her too. Clem helped put the books away. Binny's mother repacked the cupboard. James took up his train track.

"I'll never have nobody to play with it again, anyway," he said.

"Why won't you?" asked his family.

"Because now Dill's going to kill me."

"Kill you?" they said, laughing at him. "Kill you? Don't be silly, James!"

"He can't come here again. Promise you won't let him in if he tries! Clem, Mum! Binny! Promise!"

Binny promised with her fingers crossed and carried on with the tidying. It was late night before it was done, and the money was still missing. However, Max was stretched out in his basket on her bedroom floor, and in the morning he would track it down. As soon as she had it she would take it back to the bank, put up with the consequences, and ordinary life could begin again.

After three days and nights of crime, Binny longed for ordinary life. The weight of the lost money was worst when she was alone. It slowed her thoughts, so that she could concentrate on nothing else. She could not read, or write. On her bookshelf the blue notebook waited but she left it untouched. When this present trouble was over, she thought sleepily, she would write it all down, draw a line beneath the last words, turn a new page, and start again.

Chapter Nine

* * *

Tuesday Morning

Binny's mother took James with her into work the next day. She often did this; he played in the lounge or garden of the old people's home, being spoiled by the residents with sweets and stories. He went very willingly that morning, saying, "Dill can't get me there."

With James out of the house, Clem was free too. Clem was very quiet that day. This was not surprising, she nearly always was, either serene and quiet, or worried and quiet. Tuesday was one of her worried and quiet times.

"I'm going to work in the college library," she said, and vanished.

So Binny and Max had the house to themselves,

and as soon as Gareth arrived they set to work in search of the lost twenty-pound notes.

It was terribly hard.

Max could find a hidden ball.

He could find Gareth's sneakers.

He picked out Binny's notebook from a whole pile of books.

But he couldn't find money, not Gareth's, nor the notes that were missing.

He tried really hard, he knew what he was meant to do, he bounded round the house searching, but in the end he always came back to Binny and Gareth, nudging their hands in apology, asking them to help.

They gave him one of Gareth's twenty-pound notes to actually hold in his teeth. He dropped it quickly, the way he always dropped other things he didn't like in his mouth, and offered a polite paw to show that he wasn't offended.

Binny put her arms around him and said, "It's very important. Try again Max."

He looked at her worriedly, his head on one side, and then the other, understanding that she was unhappy, willing to keep trying for as long as he was asked. Eventually, when they deliberately left a corner of Gareth's note sticking out, he did manage to locate it, but that was the only time.

"He did it by sight, not by smell," said Gareth. "It's not going to work."

"It's not fair to make him keep trying either," said Binny. "He needs his walk. Let's take him out. I told you the money was gone."

"I don't know what to do," she continued, as they headed down the cliff path with a Frisbee to throw on the beach. "It's properly lost. I think it's gone to where lost things go."

"What are you on about?" demanded Gareth.

"When lost things vanish."

"Vanish where?"

"Look at Max! He loves it here! Good catch, Max! When lost things vanish to other places. You must know what I mean."

"I don't."

"You've got to have noticed. It happens quite often. You know, when you have to stop looking for something because it's disappeared forever."

"Go on," said Gareth ominously.

"I suppose there must be gaps. Ways through."

"Ways through to where?"

"Other worlds," said Binny impatiently. "Where things get lost."

Gareth had been partly watching Max, partly listening to Binny, partly picking up litter and stowing it in a carrier bag (he intended to donate his week's collection to the town art gallery as a new installation: *Public Derision, Private Despair*). Now he stopped doing everything to stare at Binny. Her nuttiness was no surprise to him, just the forms it took.

"Other worlds where things get lost?" he repeated.

"Yes," said Binny.

"What sort of things?" asked Gareth, because that seemed a slightly more simple question to ask a nutter than, *What sort of other worlds?*

"Oh," said Binny, as calmly as if they were talking about the way to the library. "Usually things that no one counts. Leaves and rocks and stuff like that. Shells," she suggested, looking down at the beach. "Rings and pencils and lids and keys. Legos," she added, thinking of James, who often lost vital parts from Lego sets. "Loads and loads of things like that and now my stolen money!"

"Bin," said Gareth incredulously. "Do you really think planet earth junk is raining down into some mythical world *through gaps*?"

"Slipping not raining."

"And I suppose their junk is coming here?"

"I suppose," agreed Binny, nodding.

"How come we never see it, then?"

Binny looked at Gareth's half full carrier bag and then down at the tideline. Bladderwrack, orange nylon string, crab claws, a curve of some sort of earthenware pot, feathers, a cube of wood hammered on all sides with mysterious blackened nails.

"Obviously it is," she said.

It surprised her to find how strongly Gareth disagreed with this sane and comforting belief. To Binny it had always been an accepted fact of life, one of the many everyday mysteries that included upside-down reflections in spoons, the shape of flames, and the Internet. Yet Gareth was almost outraged. It seemed there were no hidden gaps in his world at all. No one ever said, as they said so often in the Binny's family, *I've given up looking for my flute cleaner/the little red alarm clock/ James's other slipper.* Things given up as gone for good, for which it was no use searching anymore.

"If nothing was ever lost," said Binny, "everyone, everywhere would have piles and piles of stuff and the shops would all go bankrupt because people would only buy things like food."

But Gareth continued to gaze at her as if she had suddenly turned green, and he said very forcefully that it wasn't true, it would be on the news if it was, there were no other worlds anyway, and even if there were other worlds, there were definitely no entrances to them from their own. When Binny argued back, with examples, he appalled her by giving logical explanations for spoon reflections, flames, and the Internet.

"Bin, can't you really see what's happened?" Gareth asked.

Binny shook her head. Five minutes before Gareth's explanations she had understood. She had stolen a huge amount of money and lost it through a hole in the world. As if this wasn't bad enough, a witch had seen her take it. This had been terrible, but it had made sense at least. Now she didn't know what to think, and her only hope was Gareth, who very plainly did.

What Gareth said was shattering.

"It's clear enough. Somebody took it."

"*Took it?*"

"Yes."

"On *purpose*?"

"Yes."

"What, you think somebody came to our house and took *a whole pile of money*?"

It was a far stranger and more alarming idea to Binny than a hole in the world where things tumbled and vanished.

It was impossible.

"A burglar?" she asked at last. "A burglar, like Miss Piper thought had come yesterday, when we left the door open by mistake? That burglar? But that doesn't make sense. It was already lost by then."

Gareth smoothed the black and white fur between Max's ears, and waited.

"A burglar before that time, then?" asked Binny. "There wasn't a burglar on Sunday night. The house was all locked and you know Mum sleeps downstairs. And there wasn't a burglar the day before because that was Mum's birthday, and there were people in and out all day."

"What people?" asked Gareth.

"Clem and James and Mum and me. Dill. Pete the builder who brought a spirit level for a birthday present. Miss Piper. She gave Mum a horrible peg doll that everyone said was wonderful. Clare and her mum. They brought pink meringues with cherries on top. What are you doing, Gareth?"

Gareth had taken his mobile phone out of his pocket and was making notes. He held it out, so that Binny could read the screen.

Clem, James, Polly Cornwallis, Bin. Dill. Builder. Piper woman. Clare, Clare's mother.

"Why have you written all our names?"

"Because one of you took it."

"GARETH!"

"Obviously."

"You don't really think that!"

"I do." Gareth counted. "Nine. Nine suspects. Counting you."

"Counting me? You can't count me!"

"You stole it once," Gareth pointed out ruthlessly. "So why not count you?"

"I didn't mean to steal it. I just took it. I saw it and I took it."

"Well, that's what anyone on the list might have done."

"But I wanted it for something special!"

"So might they. Your mum must need money. Clem always does! You told me that ages ago."

"Only for her music," said Binny. "But she'd never steal it. She works in the café, you know she does. The only reason she's not doing it this vacation is because they're redecorating to get it ready for summer."

"Well then!" said Gareth. "See! Prime suspect number one!"

"No!"

"I think so. Prime suspect number two. Your mum. If your mum found money in the house she'd just assume it was hers that she'd put down and forgotten or something."

A few minutes before, Gareth had stared at Binny, marveling at her madness. Now Binny stared at him the same way.

Gareth tried to explain further: "It would be like . . . You know what it's like when you put on something you haven't worn for ages, and there's a tenner in the pocket?"

"No."

"Yes you do. And you think, 'Oh great! How long has that been there?' That's what your mum will have done. Not stealing. Just thinking it was hers that she'd put away and forgotten."

Binny shook her head at such an unlikely event.

"James and Dill, then. Could easily be them. They

were burying treasure on the beach, James said!"

"Not that sort of treasure!"

"You don't *know*!" said Gareth impatiently. "That girl Clare and her mum . . ."

"They're our friends! They'd never . . . I'm not even going to think about it! Clare is definitely not a burglar. She earns her own money. She's worked for ages for her mum, painting and cleaning to help save up for the school trip tomorrow."

"You didn't say there was a school trip tomorrow," exclaimed Gareth. "Are you going?"

"Of course not. It costs loads."

"Well then, if it costs loads and Clare's been saving, it could easily have been her that took it. Completely by accident. Saw it lying around, thought, *Oh I've dropped my money,* picked it up . . . Or her mum, if she'd been looking after it for her. It could have been either of them!"

"Never!"

"And then that Miss Piper who you said was a witch!"

"A witch! Not a burglar!"

Gareth rolled his eyes, and continued. "The builder! Pete!"

"Pete doesn't care about money. He never wants to be paid."

"'Course he does! He's got to live!"

"He lives in a caravan up on the cliffs," said Binny sulkily. "Free, if he keeps the grass and hedges cut on the caravan site. He told me."

"He still needs food, doesn't he? And diesel for his van? And tools?"

Binny glared.

"Of course, the most likely person to have it," said Gareth, "is you."

Chapter Ten

* * *

Tuesday Afternoon

The morning was passing. Binny, Gareth, and Max left the beach and followed the cliff path back home again. They lived in the oldest part of town where the streets were narrow and stony. Binny put Max back on his leash when they came in sight of the houses and she was glad that she had, because as they turned a corner he suddenly jumped, and pulled forward.

"Oh!" exclaimed Binny.

It was a dirty bundle of gray feathers huddled against a wall, one of the marketplace pigeons.

"Dead," said Binny mournfully.

"It's not," said Gareth. "I saw it move. Keep Max away." He handed Binny his bag of art installation, and twisted to yank off the hood of his parka jacket.

"Careful you don't hurt it!" said Binny anxiously, but Gareth did not need the warning. He bent over, his face focused in concentration, and then relaxed.

"There!"

The pigeon had struggled against capture at the last moment, but already it was quiet, folded into the jacket hood. Binny found herself looking at Gareth in admiration. She could not have done it, not with such steady hands and quietness. She asked, "Have you done that before?"

"Done what?" said Gareth, so Binny knew that he had, and that he would never need a school trip to find himself, because he was found already.

"Shall I put this trash in a trash can?" she asked, holding it up.

"I told you, I'm keeping it. I'm donating it to the Tate."

"It's a funny sort of art."

"It'll make people think. The whole point of art is to make people think."

"What I think, when I go to the gallery, when Clem makes me on wet Sundays," said Binny, "is I'm glad I didn't have to pay to get in. What are you going to do with the pigeon?"

"Don't know till I've had a look at it. Maybe it's just stunned. It'd better not die. You should have seen what crawled off a hedgehog that died in my hood last autumn! Not just fleas. Lice. Ticks. The minute it began to cool down . . ."

Binny moved carefully away from Gareth.

"Listen, I've got to take it home now, and see how it is, so can you come too? We'd better get going on finding that money. Will you drop off Max and come round?"

"Have you got an idea?"

"Not sure." Gareth paused to peer into his hood.

"Is it dead?"

"Not sure about that either."

"Are things crawling off it?"

"Um. Yes."

For the rest of the way home Binny and Max walked on the opposite pavement to Gareth and his pigeon.

Pete had arrived when Binny got back. "Just a thought," he had said, and now he was up in the attic, hammering so loudly the whole house echoed.

"What is it?" screeched Binny into the black square of the trapdoor.

"Plasterboard going up," replied Pete, appearing in the middle of the square, looking like a disembodied head arriving into an empty frame. "Sorry about the noise. Mrs.-next-door isn't very pleased either, although I've told her I'm nearly finished."

"Are you really?"

"Got the supports up last week. Plasterboard, plaster, finish off the wiring, fix the skylight so it opens, some sort of railing, and it'll be just right for . . ."

Pete paused and looked down at her.

". . . junk."

"Does Mum know you're nearly finished?"

"She does and she doesn't. Why do you ask?"

"Because when you're finished she'll . . ." *Have to pay you,* Binny nearly said, caught the words back just in time, and substituted, ". . . she'll . . . she'll probably . . . she'll probably miss you!"

"Oh right," said Pete, and grinned like a pirate, an expression he switched off immediately when Binny went on to ask, as casually as she could,

"How much will it cost?"

"I don't know," said Pete, not trying to hide the fact that what he really wanted to say was, *Mind your own business.* "What happened to your bedroom door?"

"It came off."

"I can see that."

"I tried to hang a hammock on it that I made out of some fishing net I found. I thought if I had a hammock then I wouldn't need a bed and I could put something else in the space."

"What's more important than a bed?"

"A desk. For writing."

"I've never heard anything so daft," said Pete, "but I'll get round to the door next time I come by."

"No!" protested Binny hurriedly. "I like it as it is. Anyway, I could easily mend it myself."

"Mend it yourself!" scoffed Pete rudely.

"I could. It only needs new hinges and a new bit of wood where the frame split off the wall. That wouldn't cost much."

Pete suddenly withdrew his head so that the picture frame emptied. The hammering began almost at once, this time with words between the whacks.

"Do you people . . . *whack*
> think of nothing . . . *whack whack*
>> but . . . *whack* . . . MONEY . . . *whack whack*
>> *whack . . . around here?"*

Money! thought Binny, and leaving Max behind she went next door to find Gareth. This took much longer than it should have, because on the way out of the house something happened. A strange, shocking encounter, which lasted less than two minutes and left Binny blinking, as if she had looked through a gap into another world.

"Why'd you take so long?" asked Gareth, pulling open the door to her when at last she arrived.

"Things happened," said Binny, following him as he led the way to the kitchen. "Miss Piper, and then I had to go back in and find Pete and then . . ."

The sight of Gareth's kitchen stopped Binny in her tracks. She said, "Gareth! They'll kill you!"

"They're out," said Gareth.

The lovely old pine table had been turned into a

mixture of an operating theater and a pigeon cleaning station. The grapes and bananas had been dumped out of the fruit bowl to make a pigeon bath. It stood, half filled with dirty water on an inadequate rectangle of newspaper. The table itself was puddly, and all among the grapes and bananas were feathers and splodges of poo.

"There'll be germs!" said Binny. "Millions I should think! She gets ill really easily too."

"Stop fussing. She's not even pregnant yet."

"How do you know?"

"I asked," said Gareth, calmly. "This morning. Don't look at me like that; I was really supportive. I said I hoped it would be twins."

"Gareth!"

"It was your idea. Come and look at the pigeon."

It was still gray and exhausted, but somehow a less awkward shape. One eye was half open and a glimmer of life shone there, weary but enduring.

"There was something like elastic hooked over its body and round under one wing and caught tight at the top of its leg. Stretchy stuff, really strong. I've managed to cut it all off. That's why there's so many feathers about. I think the black gunge on its face is chewing gum."

"Shouldn't you take it to the vet?"

"I rang them and they said to bring it in tomorrow if it lasts that long."

"Have you washed it? I think it's meant to be white."

"I only managed to get some muck off its feet, that's all. I'll get its beak clear first. It's either been trying to eat gum, or trying to preen gum off itself. It's all stuck up."

"Put it in a bag and put it in the freezer," said Binny, quoting her mother's chewing gum solution. "NO DON'T!"

Gareth rolled his eyes.

"I forgot it was alive. Gareth, I've got to tell you about Miss Piper. I've got proof now that she's a witch. She witched Pete's van right in front of me a minute ago!"

"As if!" said Gareth rudely.

"She did! Listen! When I came out to come here, she was right there on the doorstep. I thought I'd try being very polite for a change so I said I was sorry if she could hear the hammering Pete was doing in the attic—"

"That hammering's awful," interrupted Gareth. "It's why they're out. They can't stand it either. Pass me that stuff in the jug."

"What is it?"

"Olive oil. Go on about your witch, then!"

"I could see by her smile that she wasn't happy. I explained that Pete was nearly finished, but she didn't seem interested except she said that she'd been hearing he was nearly finished since before Christmas. Then she said, listen to this! Was there anything worrying me that I would like to talk to her about."

Gareth looked up and grinned.

"So I said, no, because what else could I say, and she put her head a little bit on one side and just looked at me."

"I don't know if you realize, Bin," said Gareth, "but anyone can tell if you're lying."

"That's just not true, Gareth. I'm a really good liar. Anyway, I haven't finished yet. She got really witchy after that and she said perhaps I hadn't time to consider what she meant, and meanwhile, she said, 'About your builder. I was just coming to let him know that his van is parked perilously close to the double yellow lines—'"

"Perilously!" interrupted Gareth. "No one says perilously!"

"Miss Piper did. She said perilously. So just in case she was right I went back into the house and called up the stairs to Pete and told him. Miss Piper watched me from the doorstep. I could see her there, while I called to Pete, sort of out of the edge of my eye."

"So?" asked Gareth.

"Well, Pete shouted back, 'My van? It never is! Nothing like. I checked before I left it.' All the time I was talking to Miss Piper, I could see the van behind her. But after I'd spoken to Pete, when she left, it was gone."

"What?"

"I couldn't see it anymore."

Gareth had cleared the bird's beak and nostrils. He had wiped away the grit and dust that clogged its eyes. "That's enough for now," he said, lifting it back into its cardboard box. "What happened next, then?"

"Well, the van had moved. Not far, but it was a little way down the street. So I ran back in and yelled for Pete and he came out grumbling a bit, almost straight-away, hardly anytime later, but guess what? By the time we got to it his van was right on the double yellow lines with a parking ticket on the window!"

Gareth took a while to think about that.

"He must have not put the hand brake on properly," he said at last, "and she gave it a shove."

"No she didn't. I'd have seen. And the hand brake was on when Pete got to it."

"Were the doors locked?"

"Yes."

"It's a really old van. The brakes must have slipped."

Binny shook her head. She was sure the brakes hadn't slipped. It had all happened too quickly, and too neatly to be explained with logic. She asked instead, "How much do parking tickets cost?"

"Sixty pounds round here," said Gareth promptly.

Binny seemed to go limp. "Sixty pounds!"

"Twice as much if you don't pay them straightaway. I know, my dad's an expert. He gets them all the time."

"Poor, poor Pete! Now do you believe Miss Piper is a witch?"

"No," said Gareth promptly. "His van rolled onto the yellow lines. She was pleased. Maybe she collared a traffic warden to slap a ticket on it. I can believe that much, but that's all. And I don't believe she saw you take that money."

"Why not?"

"Because if she did, what's to stop her saying, 'I, What's-her-name Piper . . .'"

"Annabelle."

". . . Okay, 'I, Annabelle Piper, saw you, Belinda Cornwallis, steal a load of money that wasn't yours and I'm a nosy old bat so I'm going to tell your mum.'"

"She hasn't said that," admitted Binny.

"No. Either because she's being very kind and giving you a chance to own up. Highly unlikely. Or because she doesn't really know the truth. She just guesses. Maybe she saw you with a handful of twenties and wondered how you could have got it. Or maybe she was around when someone came back to the ATM and said, 'Where's my money gone?' and she'd just seen you acting weird."

"Well then, why doesn't she say?"

"What, like say to your mum, 'I, Annabelle Old Bat think maybe your daughter Belinda Cornwallis stole a load of money from an ATM. I can't prove it, though, and I hope we are still friends because I really want you to give me first chance of buying your house. It would be perfect to knock through to mine and then I could tart it up for a vacation place and use it to fleece the tourists like everyone does around here.' My dad says you should sell the house. And buy something much bigger out of town a bit."

"Pete's making our house bigger anyway," said Binny. "He's making the loft so we can put junk in it."

"No wonder she witched his van," said Gareth, grinning.

"She doesn't like him, and she doesn't like me," said Binny sadly, "and I'll never get rid of her now that money is gone. I don't know what to do."

"Find it."

"How?"

Gareth got out his mobile phone, found his suspect list, and handed it to Binny.

"If you can't find out where it is, you'd better try and find out where it isn't," he said. "You'd better start eliminating people."

"Eliminating people? What do you mean, eliminating people?"

"Finding out who definitely hasn't got it. When you know all the people who definitely haven't got it, then you'll know the person who has."

Binny stared at the list, and tried to believe, as Gareth did, that on her mother's birthday, someone, perhaps accidentally, had taken that money.

It was only possible if she remembered the *perhaps accidentally*.

Then, she supposed, James and Dill really could have buried it.

Her mother actually could have discovered it as Gareth had discovered the surprise ten-pound note in his pocket.

Clem might have accidentally tidied it away.

She hated the suggestion that Pete might have taken it, but she could see why Gareth had said it.

Miss Piper was a witch, who knew what a witch might do?

Clare? Clare's mother? Binny shook her head at the thought. If anyone definitely hadn't got it, then it was them. If she had to begin eliminating people, Binny decided, they would be the easiest. She would eliminate them first.

"I'll go now," she said, at last.

"Go where?" asked Gareth.

"Out to Clare's, to eliminate them. It'll have to be today if I'm going anyway, because Clare goes away tomorrow."

"I'll come with you," offered Gareth.

"How can you?" asked Binny. "What about all this?"

"All what?"

Binny indicated the pigeon feathers, poo, poisoned fruit, soggy newspaper, and flooded kitchen table.

"I suppose you're right," said Gareth.

* * *

Clare lived a bus ride out of town, on a not-quite-making-it farm with her mother and her brother. When Binny's family had lost their roof the autumn before, they had rented the vacation house belonging to the farm until they could move back home. That had been a time of trouble and secrets for Binny and Clare, but they had managed to come out of it as friends. Very good friends, alike and unalike, two sides of a spinning coin.

Binny and Max found Clare in the vacation house, earning the last of her school trip money by painting the bare, white bathroom an even brighter and barer white.

"Mum thought it was looking a bit dark," explained Clare when she had finished hugging Max, and Binny grinned, remembering very well Clare's mother's love of bareness and whiteness.

"What else have you had to do?"

"Wash things," said Clare. "All the insides of all the cupboards and drawers. All the knives and forks and china and saucepans. All the paintwork. I've finished now. Just one last patch of bathroom wall."

"I could help you," offered Binny.

"I'd rather have a paint break," said Clare. "Come down to the kitchen. Did your mum like her birthday?"

"Yes," said Binny, following as Clare led the way. "She said she did, anyway. Clare?"

"Mmm?" asked Clare, filling the kettle.

"At my house, on Sunday, you didn't notice anything lying about, did you?"

"Only about twenty million things," said Clare cheerfully, dropping teabags into mugs and opening a packet of ginger cookies. "Can Max have one of these?"

"He'd love it."

"What's the matter? You've gone all quiet. I was only joking about the twenty million things. I like your house. It's friendly. Twenty million things lying about is good!"

"I meant money, really," mumbled Binny, blushing to say it. "Any money lying about."

"Money?" repeated Clare.

"I just wondered, if . . . I wondered if perhaps when you were at our house you saw some . . . Well, I wondered if you saw some money in a not very good place and you thought, or your mum did, you'd put it somewhere safe . . ."

Clare picked up the kettle, put it down again, changed her mind, and filled up the mugs with boiling water. She stood looking at the teabags as they swelled and floated.

"It's just that I can't seem to find . . ."

"I can't believe you just said that," said Clare.

"I didn't mean it to sound bad! I didn't mean it like it came out!"

"Me and Mum," said Clare, her voice trembly with temper. "Me and Mum, taking your money! That's what you're saying!"

"I'm not! I'm not!"

"We came to your house on Sunday to be nice! Mum made meringues! We wouldn't touch your rotten, horrible, stupid money if it was . . . if it was . . ."

"I know! I know! Of course you wouldn't!"

"Well. Good-bye." Clare picked up the two full mugs of tea, one in each hand, turned them upside down over the sink, clunked them down, and walked out of the kitchen.

"Clare!" exclaimed Binny.

"I'm sorry I won't ever see Max again," said Clare, not looking round. "But I couldn't care less about you!"

A minute later the door of the bare white bathroom was slammed very furiously shut.

Binny was stunned. To lose a friend in the time it takes to make a mug of tea. One minute, to be welcomed with ginger cookies and the next, good-bye.

"Clare!" she shouted, and ran up to the bathroom, but the door was locked and knocking brought no reply.

"What shall I do? What shall I do?" she cried to Max, but he could not help her and the door did not open.

Chapter Eleven

* * *

Tuesday Evening

Almost as soon as Binny was back from her disastrous first attempt at eliminating people, Gareth appeared, accompanied by the pigeon in its cardboard box. As so often happened, Gareth entirely failed to notice Binny's slumped unhappiness. Instead he listened to her account of the afternoon, fished his mobile from his pocket, deleted Clare and her mum from the list of suspects, and said, "Excellent!"

"It's not excellent, it's horrible. Clare is furious," said Binny.

"Bound to be," agreed Gareth, cheerfully unmoved. "Still, Max had a good walk back. Did he like the bus out?"

"Clare was my best friend," said Binny. "Now

she's never speaking to me again. Don't you care?"

"Well," said Gareth, squinting at her through his round, rather battered glasses, "not that it matters much, but I thought I was. Your best friend. In fact at school I tell people you're my girlfriend. Stops them asking if I'm gay. Do you mind?"

"Mind? Mind? Why do they ask if you're gay?"

"Haven't a clue," said Gareth dismissively. "The other good news is that the pigeon's started eating. I've got it on grated cheese and her posh muesli. I had to bring it round with me because he's in a storming temper again. He's got anger management problems but he won't go to therapy. I meant to do some tidying in the kitchen but they came back sooner than I thought they would. She said not to worry, though, so I'm not. Do you want to see it?"

"All right," said Binny, seeing that Gareth was already lifting the lid.

"What have you got there?" asked Binny's mother, passing through just then. "Oh Gareth, I don't know if I want that in here, thank you! It's not really hygienic is it? It's bad enough, having Max!"

"Max is perfectly clean!" said Binny indignantly. "Look how white his white bits are! And he doesn't smell. That bird smells."

"Max does smell," said James, coming in from the living room to look. "He smells of dog. Same as my chickens smell of chickens and Binny smells of

Binny and Gareth smells of Gareth and Clem . . ."

"I do not smell," said Clem, overhearing. "Hello Gareth!"

"Hello," said Gareth, slightly shaken, as usual, by Clem's golden-gilt shimmer, and her comprehending glance, as if she knew everything that he was thinking and it was as bad as she expected.

"I heard you'd got a pigeon," said Clem. "Into birds now, are you?"

She smiled at him so innocently that he quaked and thought, *I knew it. She can read my mind. I'll never think her name again.* Gareth would never have considered telling people at school that Clem was his girl-friend in order to stop them calling him gay, but yet, if he was ten years older, and very much taller, and could drive something amazing or maybe had a pilot's license for light aircraft, and if she would stop putting up her hair so she looked so scary . . .

He was thinking of her again. Did she know? She was still smiling.

"Can I have a look?" she asked.

"Yes all right," he agreed, rather huskily, lifting the box lid, and she looked and said, "Oh! Poor thing! A white one. I like white pigeons."

"It smells awful," said James, holding his nose. "Ponky. Worse than socks. Worse than Dill."

"That's enough of that, James!" said his mother, back again and in a rush as usual. "I'm just home for an hour, then I've got an extra shift this evening. Not for long, but . . . Binny, are you still invited out with Gareth and his family?"

"Yes, she is," answered Gareth promptly. "They said to remind her. They've booked a table at the Indian—"

Binny gave a jump of delight, James hung his tongue out in disgust, and the children's mother and Clem looked worriedly at each other.

"Well, that's lovely," said the children's mother, looking even more harassed. "You don't happen to know what time, do you Gareth?"

"No," said Gareth, then caught Clem's thoughtful eyes on him and added, "Sorry!" glanced at her again and offered (inspired), "I could go and ask," noticed her faint nod of approval, and finished, "and I'll take the pigeon home with me out of the way!" Then he exited, triumphant, on such a peak of helpful politeness that it seemed there should be a round of applause.

This did not happen. Instead, as he went out of the front door, there came a most dreadful shriek.

"I suppose one of us ought to go and see whether he's murdered someone," remarked Clem, contemplating her nails. "Or if it was just the natural reaction of a casual passerby."

Before they could investigate, however, Gareth had dumped his pigeon and was back, eager to explain for himself.

"That old woman you call Miss Piper . . . ," he began.

"It's her name!" murmured Clem. "Not just something we dreamed up."

"Miss Piper, then," said Gareth. "Her from next door, screamed when she saw me! Did you hear?"

"Is that who it was? We heard someone."

"I showed her the pigeon and it flapped and she went mental!"

"Oh, you haven't upset Miss Piper, have you?" exclaimed the children's mother, as she came in. "I wanted to ask her a favor about James!"

"About me?" asked James.

"She's often offered. It would only be for a couple of hours. Clem's got a party, she planned it ages ago. Binny's going out with Gareth's family. I've got work until nine. What about you?"

"I could go out too," said James at once. "I'm not eating curry but I could go to Clem's party."

"Of course you could," agreed Clem. "My friends would adore you!"

"See!" said James.

"It would be all big hugs and kisses!" said Clem, reaching out to demonstrate.

"I'll go with Mum, then," said James, backing away.

"Not for the evening shift," said his mother. "Not with bedtime and all the medicines to hand out."

"Max will look after James," said Binny.

"Pete might," suggested Clem.

"I'll look after myself," said ungrateful James, but

he ended up with Miss Piper, still deeply disgusted by the sight of Gareth's pigeon, but more than willing, she said, to take care of James and manage Max.

"Max won't need managing," said Binny, very distrustfully, when her mother came back from arranging this and told her the news.

"It's just her way of talking," said her mother, soothingly. "She's very kind, underneath . . ."

(Binny briefly pictured Miss Piper underneath a pointed hat.) ". . . She showed me more peg dolls she's made. They really are very clever. She's done a very sweet one of James, and she's just finishing Clem."

"I think she's got some nerve," said Binny, "pegdolling people!"

"Why couldn't I have Pete instead of Miss Piper?" demanded James. "I bet you never even asked him. He wouldn't mind. And he'd be useful. He said he'd look at Pecker and Gertie next time he was here."

The children's mother, rushing to get back to work, replied that Pete was a builder, not a babysitter, and that she was sure Miss Piper would look at Gertie and Pecker if she was invited very politely. Then she kissed him (protesting) on the top of his head, and ran.

"I'll have to ask Miss Piper, then," said James crossly to Binny when his mother was gone. "Someone's got to look at Pecker and Gertie. They've got nits."

The thought of Miss Piper being invited to look at Pecker and Gertie's nits stopped Binny worrying about

Max while she was out with Gareth and his family. Miss Piper, she guessed, would be far too busy to notice him. It was disappointing to return home and find James very firmly asleep in bed, his slippers lined up with unnatural neatness, his clothes on his bedroom chair, folded as they had seldom been folded before. Max was curled tightly in his basket under the kitchen table, and in the garden Gertie and Pecker were crooning placidly, their feathers unruffled and their nits, it seemed, undisturbed.

"What happened with Miss Piper?" she asked her mother, who was home by then.

"Nothing at all," said her mother, smiling. "Everyone as good as gold, I gather. Was it fun this evening?"

"We had papadums and there were rose petals on the stairs. One petal on each side of every stair, all the way up. My rice had almonds in it and there were little silver dishes all over the table. Not real silver, but still. Did you have to work very hard with the old ladies?"

"Not very. Just helping people to bed and things."

"Things," said Binny, groaning.

"Binny, I like my job," said her mother firmly. "I like the kind, brave, funny people I meet. As I have told you a hundred times before! I have had a nice day. What about you?"

For Binny, already the rose petal and papadum sparkle was fading fast. It vanished completely as she remembered her day. *I made a suspect list with Gareth. I annoyed Pete by talking about money. I saw Miss*

Piper witching in the street. I eliminated Clare. "It's lovely having Max here," she said diplomatically.

"It is," agreed her mother.

"Are you staying up till Clem comes home?"

"Perhaps. But you should go to bed, Binny."

"Can I read if I do?"

"Of course. And I'll be up in a few minutes to say good night. Do you remember the TuckyUp Monster?"

The TuckyUp Monster had been the children's mother, transformed into monstrousness when the clock struck eight. It had lumbered up the stairs and into the shrieking children's bedrooms, roaring "TuckyUp! TuckyUp! TuckyUp!" It tucked them in tight and hugged them, in the bedtimes of long ago.

"I used to love the TuckyUp Monster," said Binny, and when she went upstairs she chose an old book from TuckyUp Monster days, *Five on a Treasure Island.* Soon she was so lost in the world of the Famous Five and Timmy the dog that she jumped when her mother tapped on her bedroom door, and then pushed it open.

"Binny, Bin, Belinda, Bel," she said, as she sat down on the end of the bed, "and Max." She reached down to rub him between his ears. "How do you like having a bedroom door again?"

"I didn't notice I had until you knocked on it just then."

"Wasted on you! What's the book?"

"I'm too old for it really." Binny turned it so that her mother could see the cover.

"Ah!" her mother said. "I remember that one! The castle on the island and the dungeons full of gold ingots!"

Binny nodded.

"Why did you hang a hammock onto your door in the first place? Pete tried to explain, but it didn't seem to make much sense."

The hammock idea seemed so far in the past now that for a moment Binny struggled to remember. "I thought that if I could manage without a bed I could make space for a desk," she said eventually. "A desk or a table. Something big and flat to write on. I thought I'd rather have a desk than a bed and there isn't room for both. It doesn't matter now."

Her mother looked at her thoughtfully, but did not ask, "Why not?"

"Your dad had a lovely desk," she said instead. "You used to make dens underneath it when you were very little. Do you remember?"

"Mum?"

"Yes?"

"Dad is *dead* isn't he?"

"Binny! Yes. Yes he is."

"I was just checking. In case it was like in old books and it turns out they were only in prison or had brain fever or their airplane crashed on a deserted island."

"Yes, I understand, Binny."

"What happened to Dad's desk?"

"It's in storage. I didn't want to part with it, but it's too big for anywhere we've lived since. Maybe one day we'll have space for it."

"You don't want to move house again, do you?" Binny asked, alarmed, but even as she spoke she knew it was not a fair question to ask someone who slept on the sofa, kept her two dresses in Clem's wardrobe, and all her other clothes and things in the narrow darkness of the cupboard under the stairs. Very recently Pete had said, "Just a thought," and put a light in the cupboard. "Luxury!" Binny's mother had exclaimed, and the cry of, "Who has borrowed my flashlight?" was no longer heard.

But it isn't really luxury, thought Binny. It would be much better for her mother if they did move house.

"I could swap rooms with you if you like, Mum!" she offered now. "Would that be better?"

"I don't think it would," said her mother, hugging her and laughing. "I'll think we'll stay as we are for the moment."

"If you change your mind I will."

"Thank you, but meanwhile I can manage without a bedroom if you can manage without a desk. What are you writing now, Binny?"

"I'm not really writing anything."

"You finished the Max biography, didn't you? I

thought you'd be filling up your Little Prince notebook."

Binny shook her head. Writing frightening things down made them far too clear to bear. She had lost her writing escape as surely as she had lost the money.

"What's the matter, Binny?"

"Nothing."

"Not true. Dad?"

"I should never have asked you that about Dad."

"You can always ask me anything about Dad, Binny," said her mother, so Binny asked the question that she had wondered for years.

"Do you think he knew before he died that we would be bankrupt?"

"I think," said her mother, after a very long pause, "he always believed that something magical would come along and save it all. I am sure he never guessed, for instance, that you would lose Max."

Max beat his tail at the sound of his name, and they both looked at him with love.

"I found him again," said Binny, comfortingly, seeing the sadness on her mother's face.

"Yes," her mother agreed, but her face was still sad, and since cheerfulness hadn't helped, Binny tried a plain unreasonable grumble instead.

"I told Pete I didn't mind not having a door. I even said I liked it better, but he's fixed it all the same."

It worked. Her mother stopped looking sad and became indignant.

"It's not a problem to most people, Binny, having a bedroom door. If it really annoys you I suppose we could ask him to take it off again."

"Then we'll have to pay him even more!" said Binny. "He's done millions of things now, not just mending the roof. How will we pay him for them all?"

"You're worrying about money!" exclaimed her mother. "That's what it has been all this week! Oh Binny! It hardly took Pete and me ten minutes to fix your door. It was fun! We leveled it with my birthday spirit level! Don't think about it for one minute more!"

"But he still needs to be paid," said Binny, stubbornly. "He still needs things," she added, remembering Gareth's words, "food and tools and diesel for his van."

"You really have been thinking about it!" said her mother. "I knew there was something wrong. Money! I thought it was much worse than that! Come on, give me a hug and say, 'Mum, I'm so not worried about money that if I find a dungeon full of gold ingots, I won't bother to bring them home!'"

That was so close to the awful truth that Binny could hardly bear it.

"What would you do if I did?" she asked.

"Take them to the police station and say, "'My very strong daughter has managed to carry these gold ingots home. Please would you find the owner.'" But you never would. You'd have more sense!"

Chapter Twelve

★ ★ ★

Wednesday Morning, Part One

Wham are you doing?" asked James, up before seven the next morning and peering at Binny in the bathroom. "What's that smell?"

"Go away! You should knock, not just barge in!"

"I don't knock," said James, as if stating a truth beyond his control. "Your hair's dripping brown drips."

Binny mopped anxiously. Brown splodges appeared on her towel.

"Why are you washing your hair with dirty shampoo?" asked James.

"It's not shampoo."

"Why are you putting it on your head, then?"

"To change the color. I'm tired of looking like

seaweed. What are you doing here anyway?"

"My toothpaste cooking." James squirted a dollop of mint toothpaste onto the tip of a finger and looked at it consideringly. "Strawberry sauce?" he inquired of his reflection in the mirror. "Oh yes, thank you!" he replied, nodding politely, and added a swirl of Peppa Pig pink.

"Pudding!" he announced, between delicate cat licks.

"No wonder the toothpaste is used up all the time!" said Binny.

"I know. Especially the strawberry," said James shamelessly. "Do you want to see my muscles?"

He pulled up his pajama top to display a set of bony ridges that Binny correctly identified as ribs. "Ribs are good too," she told him consolingly, when he looked disappointed.

"Good as muscles?"

"Definitely. They stop you caving in."

"What do muscles do?"

"Stop you falling apart."

"Wow," said James, and made another pudding to celebrate.

"What happened with Miss Piper last night?" asked Binny.

"It was very polite," said James, after some thoughtful licking. "She said very polite things for me to do and then I very politely did them."

"What sort of things?"

"'Please pick those clothes up.' So I did. And 'Please go to bed.' So I went."

This was such an unusual description of her brother at bedtime that Binny looked at him carefully, checking for bewitchment. She would have asked more questions if James had not innocently remarked that it was taking ages for her hair to be done.

Binny had equipped herself with an alarm clock and then forgotten to use it. Now, after a horrified glance in the bathroom mirror, she shrieked, "Get out of the way! Get out of the way!" and hung her head over the side of the bath with the shower on full. Dreadful colored water streamed from her head.

"Have you changed your mind?" asked James.

"Shampoo!" ordered Binny, groping and blind.

James passed it, and the bubbles turned gray.

"It's like when we studied about pollution at school," he said, watching with interest as she drowned.

"Towel! Towel!" begged Binny, reaching out from the deluge. "There! It's done! I've done it! I knew I could!"

"Have you?" asked James, and he looked first at the picture of the extremely dry and glamorous person on the hair dye box, and then at Binny, drenched to her waist, and so far from glamorousness as to have dyed her ears brown.

"Yes, definitely," said Binny.

"What color is it going to be? Different to seaweed?"

"Urban Darkness," said Binny, proudly. "Much different to seaweed, you'll see!"

It was Gareth who had first looked at Binny's crinkly hair and described it as seaweed colored. "Not green seaweed," he had explained, as if that made it any better. "The red stuff you get at very low tides. Or washed up," he had added helpfully.

It was an unusual description, but Binny, after privately inspecting a piece of washed up red seaweed herself, had decided he was right. Months later, wandering round the Pound Shop, she had noticed and bought a box of dark hair dye, half price because it was squashed. She had kept this secret for ages; it might have stayed hidden forever if Miss Piper had not made a peg doll that looked so knowingly like her it made her shiver to remember. Not any longer, though. Clem's old pink shirt was buried deep in the linen basket, and the notebook was abandoned. The peg doll's jeans had puzzled her until she remembered that it was supposed to be spring. She had hacked her own jeans into shorts and endured the icy consequences. And now, to finish the transformation, her hair was no longer a seaweed knot. It was a great cloud of Urban Darkness.

Her mother saw it first.

"Show me the box!" she said, the moment Binny appeared, but after she had looked at it she relaxed and hugged her, and said she'd wondered what all the splashing was about.

"Did you hardly recognize me?" asked Binny so hopefully her mother laughed and said, "Do you know, I hardly did, you look so different."

It was too different for Clem.

"You idiot! Your gorgeous hair!" she exclaimed.

Binny was so astonished that she stared.

"You always laughed at it!"

"Yes, but still, that amazing color!"

"Twenty-four washes and it will be amazing again," her mother told her soothingly.

Binny began to feel a little indignant, like someone who had been cheated of something valuable that they never knew they owned.

"That new color reminds me of our fence," remarked James. "The bit at the end of our garden where I used to—"

"Thank you *very* much *James*. That's *enough*," said his mother.

"It's just the same color. Fence brown."

"It's Urban Darkness," said Binny quite crossly. "So you shut up!"

Binny went out to meet Gareth with her Urban Darkness fence brown hair dangling loose around her shoulders like a brown tattered veil, and the moment she stepped out of the front door Miss Piper appeared.

"Ah," she said, with her head very slightly on one side. "A new look?"

"Yes," said Binny.

"Very different."

"Good."

"Shorts! My goodness!"

"It's spring," said Binny.

"No notebook either, and no pink shirt," said Miss Piper, turning up her mouth in a lipstick smile. She was dressed in pink herself that morning; soft pink and silvery pink earrings. A disguise, thought Binny, edging toward Gareth's door. A disguise which won't work because I know she's a witch.

"Before you go," said Miss Piper, smiling a rose pink smile and at the same time holding Binny back by invisible witchstrings, "I have a little gift for you . . . oh, nothing of any value," she added, seeing the look of horror on Binny's face. "Just something that might amuse, or have amused, before you changed so quickly. Come over and wait for a moment while I find it!"

Because she couldn't think of a way of avoiding it, Binny hovered uncomfortably on Miss Piper's doorstep, while Miss Piper, from somewhere beyond her front door, made time wasting remarks about pigeons, builders, and the purple honesty plants which she had growing in her garden and which were not as strong as she would like.

"Oh," said Binny.

"Tell me, how is your builder getting on?" called Miss Piper. "I can't help wondering how much longer he is going to make that job last."

"He's not always here," said Binny. "And he tries not to bother you with his van. He often parks right up the street and carries things down."

"Yes, I have noticed," said Miss Piper, her smile curving a little higher. "Why the change?"

"He says he's had enough of parking tickets and flat tires and batteries gone dead . . ."

Binny stopped, midsentence. Miss Piper had moved so Binny had a sudden glimpse of her hall table. On it was a silver framed photograph of the Queen aged seven, a vase of silvery leaves, and a toy that might have belonged to James, a small white van. It was a miniature, rather cleaner, version of Pete's.

All the magic that Binny half believed in, witches and openings between worlds, came rushing back to her as she stared.

Pete's van.

"*No wonder!*" said Binny, when her breath came back, and Miss Piper, following her gaze, said, "Yes. It makes me smile."

"Smile!"

"Quite a nice little model. It has a charm."

"A charm!"

"There beneath the honesty! Those silvery leaves are

named honesty, by the way Binny! Yes, a charm that is rather lacking in the original, I am sorry to say. And speaking of charms, this is what I meant for you. Hold out your hand!"

"And it was Max!" Binny told Gareth, when at last the two of them hurried out with Max together. "Max! And she said, 'Keep him safe!'"

"Show me again," ordered Gareth, slowing up. "I didn't see properly before."

It was a tiny model from an old toy farm, a black and white sheepdog, cast in metal, and although the paint was worn in places it was very like prick eared, banner tailed Max.

"She said she found it on a market stall," said Binny. "She found Pete's van there too, she told me. I've told you how she witches his van. She could have done anything to Max!"

Gareth rolled his eyes.

"You know why she gave it to me? And why she let me see the van? It was a warning! Showing me what she could do. What does she know about the money? What does she know? Are you scared of her, Gareth?"

"No I'm not!" said Gareth with a snort of disgust. "She's just dotty, that's all. What's the matter with your hair?"

"I dyed it so as not to look like her horrible peg doll."

"It was better like it was."

"Not you as well! You always said it was seaweed colored!"

"Still is," said Gareth, as they reached the beach. "Just a different sort of seaweed. You're more bladder-wrack now!"

He held up a strand to show her.

"Oh shut up!" said Binny. "Come on, let's keep moving or we'll freeze! There's a Coke can in that rock pool, right in the deepest bit. Are you going to get it for your art?"

For a moment Gareth looked ungrateful for this suggestion. It wasn't the weather for rock pool diving.

"Perhaps it doesn't matter," said Binny, and such an ignorant remark was the help her friend needed to strip off his jacket and his hoodie, push up his T-shirt sleeve, and plunge his arm in shoulder high.

"You might as well get the potato chip packet too, now you're soaked," said Binny, pointing.

Gareth dived again.

"Is it cold?"

"Bone aching. Pass me the trash bag! What do you want to do when we get back?"

"Find that money," said Binny. "Find it, get rid of it, and never have to think about it again."

"Okay," said Gareth. "We'll carry on eliminating people. Not Clare or her mother, you say."

"No."

"Your mum?"

"No," said Binny. "We talked about money last night. She'd have said. I know she would. She told everyone when she found ten pounds behind the clock."

"All right. That leaves old Piper, James and Dill, you, Pete. Clem. It won't be Clem, obviously."

Binny looked at him in surprise. Clem hadn't been let off so easily the first time that he had made his list.

"Obviously?" asked Binny.

"Clem's not the sort to go grabbing at money."

"I thought you didn't like her much. I thought she . . ." Binny broke off suddenly.

"What?"

"Scared you!"

"*Scared me?*" asked Gareth.

"Being so grown-up."

"No she's not."

"And pretty."

"Can't say I noticed."

"And clever."

"I don't find intelligent people frightening," said Gareth in a very annoyed voice. "Stupid ones, definitely. Anyway, of course I like her. She was really nice about my pigeon."

Despite her worries, Binny grinned, although at the same time she felt a flicker of uncertainty. Gareth was wrong. Of all of them, Clem was by far the most likely to grab at money. Over and over again, Binny had witnessed her sister's ruthlessness when it came to finding the way to pay for the music that mattered so much. And Clem was not herself these last few days.

"What about Pete?" asked Gareth, interrupting these thoughts. "A lot of people would guess Pete."

"I wouldn't. I don't want it to be him."

"Who'd you want it to be, then?"

"Miss Piper, but it isn't, or else why is she dropping such horrible hints all the time?" Binny paused to throw Max's ball for him. "Anyway, she's a witch, not a burglar. She's got a broomstick, did I tell you? An actual broomstick! I've seen it in her garden!"

Gareth grinned.

"I'm not joking!"

"I know. That's what's funny."

"Anyway, Miss Piper doesn't need to be a burglar. She's rich enough already."

"Rich!" scoffed Gareth. "Who says?"

"Pete says. I heard Pete telling Mum how she owns loads of the vacation cottages around here. And Clem says she's rich too, because she has so many cashmere cardigans."

"So what?"

"They are very, very expensive."

"Oh. Well anyway," said Gareth, sensibly dismissing cashmere cardigan fashion, which was not his strongest subject, "you've forgotten James and Dill. What if the treasure they buried was your twenty-pound notes?"

"They couldn't be so stupid."

"Of course they could! James could be that stupid on his own, never mind with Dill to help."

Binny looked at him doubtfully.

"Remember when he dropped that door key in the harbor on purpose!" said Gareth.

"That was a long time ago."

"And when he put the chicken in the attic! When he grew poisonous salad and tried it out on me! What about the time he mended Clare's mum's TV!"

"I didn't know you knew about that."

"He told me himself."

"You see! He told you! James is honest. He would never have taken the money."

"He stole that chicken last summer, that wasn't very honest!"

"He didn't steal it! He swapped it for things he had."

"I know! Stuff he got from the old ladies where your mum works! That ring! The watch and the ruby!"

"He thought they didn't want them anymore. Anyway, he would never take money. He wouldn't know what to do with it if he had it. He once had five pounds and it muddled him up so much he cried."

"I bet he wouldn't cry now," said Gareth. "I bet he'd love a load of money. I bet he'd know what to do with it too. I'll ask him!"

"Be careful!" said Binny alarmed. "Don't let him guess why you're asking, in case he tells Mum and Clem."

Gareth said he would be careful, a lot more careful

than Binny had been with Clare. He wasted no time getting on with his questioning. As soon as he and Binny got back he invited James to come and witness the pigeon's morning bath.

Very soon afterward, by means of devious and skillful questioning, he discovered exactly how James would deal with a great deal of money.

"You couldn't just spend it," said James. "Because they'd all say, 'Where did you get it from?' You'd have to hide it and spend it in little bits. What are you doing?"

Gareth, who was suddenly adding exclamation marks after James's name on the Suspects list, said, "Nothing, nothing. Go on."

"But if I had a lot of money I didn't have to hide or spend in little tiny bits," James continued obediently, "I'd buy a suit of armor and kill Dill."

"*What?*"

"I'd buy a suit of armor and kill Dill," repeated James placidly.

"But Dill's your friend!"

"Not anymore."

"Anyway, you couldn't. You couldn't kill anyone with a suit of armor."

"With a sword you could. Or a *Star Wars* lightsaber."

"But why do you want to kill Dill?"

"I don't want to, I just have to. To stop him killing me."

The pigeon had finished its bath. Each time the water was less murky. Each time its wings were stronger. Now it attempted to preen its tattered feathers and Gareth looked at it with pride. Early that morning he had taken it to the vet, borrowed a cage, and been given some advice. Now he carried the pigeon in its cage out to the garden and scattered birdseed over the lawn.

"Other pigeons will come," he explained to James, "so when I let it go it'll have a flock to fly off with. That wing was only bruised. The vet said to give it a couple of days and then let it try and leave. Come on, then! Tell me about you and Dill."

"He's turned into my enemy. He's waiting for a chance to get me."

"Oh come on, James! Don't be so daft!"

"He stares at me out of his grandma's window. Every time I go and see if he's still there, he is. Waiting."

Gareth demanded proof of this, and straightaway was led into the street and along to Dill's grandmother's house. Sure enough, there at the window stood Dill, white faced, motionless, glaring at James with murderous burning eyes.

"He's always there now," said James.

"What, standing there, just like that?"

"Sometimes he blinks. Not often."

All at once, Dill sprang into action and mimed terrible chopping and very high kicks.

"That was his kung fu fighting," said James, when, as suddenly as he had begun, Dill became motionless again. "He does that too, as well as the staring."

"When did this all start?" asked Gareth.

"After he saw *Kung Fu Panda*."

"No, no, when did the staring out of the window thing start?"

"That day we went to the beach."

"Ah!" said Gareth. "Burying treasure. Is that right?"

James nodded. "Come away now," he urged, backing up as he spoke and tugging on Gareth's arm to make him follow. "Don't talk so loud; I think he can hear through glass. And don't wave! It makes him madder."

Gareth allowed himself to be towed backward until they reached James's doorstep and then he asked, "Why did your treasure burying cause so much trouble?"

"It was meant to be a secret," James explained. "A deafly secret . . ." (He paused to touch his ears. Still working. Good.) "Both of us were going to bury secret things. It was Dill's idea and then he spoiled it."

"How?"

"He guessed what I buried," said James, round eyed and solemn. "That's why he's so mad."

"So did you bury something of his, then?"

James sighed regretfully, and glanced over his shoulder.

"Well," said Gareth cunningly, "I suppose he buried something of yours, didn't he? So that's fair. As long as neither of you buried something really stupid, like a whole lot of money."

"It was a secret, what Dill buried."

James's voice was getting smaller and smaller as he spoke, while his ears glowed scarlet with guilt.

"You know what it was," said Gareth sternly.

"It was in a tin," said James. "A special red coffee tin with bare ladies on it."

"Bare what?" asked Gareth, rather startled.

"Ladies. Gold bare ladies."

There was a sudden movement at Dill's grandmother's window. The kung fu fighting had started again. James lost courage completely and bolted into the house. Gareth found him five minutes later, deep behind the sofa.

"Come out!" he commanded, peering round at him, but James only put his fingers in his ears and screwed his eyes tight shut.

Chapter Thirteen

✳ ✳ ✳

Wednesday Morning, Part Two

While Gareth and James were watching the phenomenon of Dill in the window, Binny had gone into the house to find Pete, very much at home, making tea in the kitchen.

"One for your mum before she goes to work," he said. "I'll take it out to the garden for her in a minute. One for me. One for you if you want it. One for Clem, take it up to her, will you Bin, and tell her I'm going to have to turn the power off for half an hour or so."

"Why are you?"

"So I don't get frazzled in the attic setting up lighting for the family masterpiece."

"We haven't got a family masterpiece."

"You've got everything but, though," said Pete,

looking meaningfully at the pile of junk Binny had dropped when she came in the door: jacket, dog leash, plastic bag of beach trash for Gareth's art installation, chewed Frisbee, and sandy sneakers.

"It's hard to know where to put it all," said Binny.

"Coat peg, coat peg, trash can, dog basket, outside till they dry then bang them together to get the sand off and shoe box by the back door.

Binny gave him one of her looks.

"And don't let that tea get cold!" said Pete, and strode outside.

Bossy, thought Binny, redistributing her heap nevertheless. She could see him through the kitchen window, being watched admiringly by her mother while he did something outrageous to Gertie.

"*Nit powder!*" mouthed her mother, seeing Binny looking, and gave her a double thumbs-up. Binny returned the thumbs-up rather limply, feeling that nit powder was not a thing to be celebrated with such joy.

"I've brought you a cup of tea from Pete," she called to Clem as she climbed the stairs. "And he said to tell you he's turning the power off. Where are you?"

"Bathroom. I know he's turning the power off. I'm having a shower before he does. Put the tea in my bedroom!"

"*Please!*" said Binny reprovingly.

"Please!"

"Okay."

Binny turned the handle of Clem's bedroom door and went in and, as she always did when she found herself there, paused to gaze around.

It was quite unlike any other part of the house, or for that matter, any part of any other house that Binny had ever seen. Once, in the days when she still wrote things down to untangle them, she had searched for a whole evening to find the best way to express the mystery that her sister had created in that room. In the end, she had decided upon snow. Clem's room had the same feeling as a landscape after snowfall. The clutter of the everyday world was gone, and the light was clear.

Clem achieved her snowscape bedroom by owning very little. Her clothes were so few that they hardly filled her narrow chest of drawers. There was nothing in her bookcase except a few books from the college library, her college notebooks, and a pile of music. A miniature table worked for a desk, just big enough for a friend's discarded laptop and two pens and a pencil in a tub. There was a bed, a music stand, a small mirror, and a silvery shell on the windowsill and that was all.

Out of this place of calm came sound. An enormous quantity of sound, that raced and raged and cascaded and flowed through the white closed door, created by the only possession Clem owned that she really treasured: her silver flute.

Clem's flute was the explanation for her room. The shattering cost of specialist flute lessons was the reason for the emptiness of the chest of drawers, the spaces in the bookshelf, and the ancient laptop. Binny could never have lived like that, but all the same she loved to stand and admire the result.

This time, however, Binny gazed around the room and she was puzzled. It had changed. The whole feeling was different, as different as the house had been when the roof blew off. Yet, there was the bed and the table and the chair. The books and music and the shell and the mirror were all in place. Binny turned, taking it all in, wondering.

The chest of drawers.

James and Binny and the children's mother constantly left their possessions lying about, but Clem never did and her flute least of all. If it wasn't in her hands, it was safely in its case on top of the chest of drawers.

Now it wasn't there.

When had Clem last played her flute? Binny clutched her head to think. Not today, she knew, nor yesterday, she was sure.

Monday!

The day of the lost money and the frantic hunt. The day of the noises like lunatic owls and Clem's oblivious passing through the chaos, leaving Binny the grown-up and James and Dill free to escape with their treasure to the beach. And she had run after them, leaving the door wide open behind.

Binny's skittering thoughts were never far from the furthest reach of possibility that Gareth called unreal. Clem's flute was absent; was it lost? Surely, surely, surely, it had not fallen through the same gap in the world that had taken the money?

Had Miss Piper's first guess been correct, then? Had they been burgled after all?

No, thought Binny, coming to her senses. If either of those things, lost or stolen, had happened to the flute, Clem would have dismantled the universe to find it.

While Binny stood looking, there came the click of the bathroom door opening, and then Clem was in the doorway, her hair wrapped up in a towel, and her eyebrows a little raised to indicate that she was surprised to find Binny still in her room.

"Thank you," she said, removing the mug of tea Binny still held. "I'm going to get dressed now, so off you pop."

"Clem, where's your flute?" said Binny.

Clem became very still.

"Is it stolen? Lost?"

"No."

"Where, then? You haven't . . . you can't have sold it?"

"No NO! Of course not!" Clem closed the door behind her and leaned her back against it. "It's gone to be mended, that's all."

"Oh!" All at once Binny understood the terrible owl noises. "It was broken? Why didn't you say?"

Clem ignored that question and went on. "The music department at college helped. They know a place, so that's where we've sent it. It's out of alignment . . . it's not an enormous problem."

"Will it cost much to be fixed?"

"My flute teacher talked to them. That made it a bit less. It'll be back in a few days. Don't tell Mum."

"Why not?"

"Because there's no need for fuss."

"But what about paying, Clem? How will you manage?"

"It's paid for already," said Clem, calmly, but she would not look at Binny as she spoke.

Binny left Clem's room, stood on the landing, thought, and then bounded back.

"Clem, where did you get the money to pay for your flute?"

There was a pause while Binny waited and Clem's eyes grew wide with outrage.

"That is absolutely none of your business," she said, at last.

"It might be," said Binny.

"How?"

"Like when you sell things?"

"How is that your business?"

Binny hesitated. There was a regret about Clem's selling that she had felt for years and never mentioned "When they are things I might have had, it is."

"What absolute nerve!" exclaimed Clem.

"It's true. Lots of my friends get things passed on from their big sisters. And if you are going to say, 'What about the ones without big sisters like Clare,' well, they get the things new themselves in the first place. Ella has a bike that she had from her big sister and Clare has a bike that her mum got her new. But you sold yours."

"Why shouldn't I have sold it?" demanded Clem. "It was mine. I had it for my birthday when I was eleven or twelve or something. It was a *present*!"

"I didn't have a bike for a present when I was eleven or twelve or something."

"That's because things were different by then."

"If I had," continued Binny, "I could go and see Clare when I liked without waiting for buses. Gareth and I could go biking together."

"I had to have the money, Binny."

"You sold your ice skates and your Rollerblades. Loads of clothes and books. That little camera you had for your ski trip. All your camping things from when you used to go with Guides. I expect lots of other things I don't know too. All the stuff you had when you were the eldest and we hadn't gone bankrupt. So I think it is my business. And that's why I asked about the money for your flute."

"Do you think I like it?" snapped Clem in a furious whisper. "I hate it! I always have. Selling special things. Putting up notices at school when Dad had only just died. Lying in shops about my age. Asking my friends!"

"Okay. Shut up."

"It was the only way I could carry on learning. Mum couldn't earn enough. I couldn't earn enough. I admit it, I'm selfish."

Clem's anger was all gone. She sat slumped at her desk with her head in her hands. She rubbed her eyes with the damp towel that was unwinding from her head and said, "I'm sorry, Binny."

Binny, rubbing her hot cheek against Clem's damp hair, became the comforter.

"I'm sorry too. The bike and everything, I shouldn't have said. And it's not always like that anyway. Remember the dolls' house, ages ago? I made such a fuss and you didn't sell it."

"We've been falling over it ever since," said Clem, sniffing a bit but hugging her back. "I wish I could have kept the bike for you. But I couldn't. The only thing I can do properly, almost properly, is play the flute."

"It's not!" exclaimed Binny. "You can do millions of things! You're clever! You're pretty! If your worst thing wasn't having your photo taken, you could be a model!"

"A model! No thank you!" said Clem, laughing now. "You be a model, if you want a model in the family! Oh Binny, look at you. Why did you dye your seaweed hair?"

"Gareth says it still is seaweed. Bladderwrack, he says."

"As soon as I'm rich I'll buy you a bike."

"I'd rather have a car, thank you, Clem. With a top that folds down like Gareth's dad's."

"What color?"

"Probably green. I think Max would like green too."

So they were friends again, and a little more equally than before. Clem, the dazzling big sister had said, "I'm selfish."

And I looked after her, thought Binny, remembering Clem's defeated shoulders as she sat at her desk. That's fair, she admitted, and her mind went back to the hundreds of times that Clem had been there for her. *When I had nightmares every night. When Mum wasn't there when I got home from school. When I had chicken pox and Mum still had to go to work. When she made Max a birthday cake and it was cheese with ham icing.*

Clem isn't selfish, thought Binny, but where did the money come from to mend the flute?

I can't ask her again.

The children's mother called up the stairs that she was just on her way to work and there were sandwiches in the kitchen for anyone who wanted them, and lentil soup on the stove because it was such a cold day. Binny ran down to say good-bye, and then Max became so excited at the sight of shoes going on and coats being found that Binny put him on his leash.

"We'll walk with you to keep you company," she told her mother.

"Lovely."

They set off together, in the opposite direction to
Dill's grandmother's house, past Miss Piper's flowery,
lacy, waiting windows, past the baker's on the corner,
where the pasties were piled in the window like a har-
vest. Then along down the narrow street and into the
marketplace. From there they had a view of the sea,
wave shaken right to the horizon. A row of herring
gulls stood along the library roof, their backs to the
wind, their yellow eyes half closed, concentrating furiously on changing the weather by the power of herring
gull thought.

"Dreaming of summer," said Binny's mother.

"And tourists and fries," agreed Binny. "And being
able to put down both feet without freezing."

"Overflowing trash cans and toddlers' ice creams
and sandwiches dropped in the sand."

"Photo opportunities down at the harbor," said
Binny. "And when the rocks are warm to touch, and the
water is so calm they can balance on the lobster pot
buoys and stretch out a wing without wobbling."

"Where's your notebook?" asked her mother.

"At home somewhere."

"Here's a pen," said her mother, scrabbling in her
bag. "And here's the water bill envelope. Find somewhere to sit before you forget and write down the
herring gull dreams! I've got to rush."

Binny didn't rush. She made her way along the
sandy, windy promenade that led to the harbor and

hunkered down by the lobster pots and diesel cans, and then for ten blissful chilly minutes she recorded the herring gulls' dreams of summer. Afterward she walked home again with the wind at her back and Max, warm and companionable against her bare leg, searching her mind for a word to capture the chilly, broken brightness of the sea, and so completely happy that she passed Miss Piper's lace curtains without noticing or flinching.

Binny's own home had no lace curtains. Nobody in the Cornwallis family minded who looked in their windows. Quite often they did it themselves, even James, standing on tiptoe to peer through the panes for another point of view.

That was how Binny came to see Pete.

Pete, alone in the living room, holding her mother's bag, not the scruffy bright bag that she took to the old people's home when she went to work, but the big squashy drawstring shoulder bag on the long strap that she loved, that she had had all Binny's life, and before. Worn green leather, supple as velvet, lined with greeny blue watered silk, and smelling faintly of perfume spilled years before. Inside a Christmas stocking collection of treasures. Binny knew them well, having seen them produced so often: the silver comb, the small packet of photos, the pencil from her school days with her name, POLLY KNIGHT. The turquoise enamel compact with the silver bow catch, the dinosaur Band-Aids for when James fell down. And as well as these things, and others too, the housekeeping money in its much tried, overworked but never quite exhausted bulgy brown purse.

Just like their father's briefcase, this bag was private. Even though they saw it every day. Nobody, not even James, had ever needed to be told that people who sleep on a sofa and keep their clothes in the cupboard under the stairs need some little space that is theirs alone.

The drawstring was loose. Pete's right hand was in the bag. All this Binny saw in a moment, and her heart went still with shock.

She looked again, and the scene had changed. There was no one in the room. The bag lay undisturbed on the armchair in the corner. From somewhere very close behind, Miss Piper's voice said, "I'm going to have to hurry you, Binny."

Chapter Fourteen

★ ★ ★

Wednesday Afternoon

The whole of Binny leaped with shock. She launched straight into panic-stricken flight. Gareth's father, opening his front door at the critical moment, took the impact directly in his chest.

"Oy!" he called, seizing Max's leash as Binny pushed past him and shot by, but she was already in his kitchen. She tumbled to a halt in front of Gareth's stepmother, dreamily smiling over her coffee and feeling much less wicked than usual.

"Binny!" she exclaimed.

Binny stared speechlessly into her face.

"Whatever is the matter? Come here, sit down."

Binny felt a gentle hand between her shoulders, and allowed herself to be guided to a chair.

"Goodness, you look cold! I'm going to put Gareth's jacket around your shoulders . . . like this . . . It smells a bit of burnt toast but never mind that . . . There now! I'm going to make you some hot chocolate. I've got milk heated already, so it won't take a moment. Can you help yourself to shortbread? You won't believe it Binny, but I was just thinking about you a moment ago. You've been such a help . . . I'll tell you one day . . . Now then, drink this!"

Already Binny was thawing, inside and out. The unexpected welcome, together with Gareth's toast-smelling, down filled jacket, was wonderfully comforting. The hot chocolate tasted of kindness. Binny hugged the mug in her hands, and breathed in the warmth.

"Thank you," she said, and she was smiling over the rim at her when Gareth's father came in, with Gareth behind him.

"Max is back at your house," said Gareth. "I've just taken him round. Are you mad, bringing him here?"

"I'm sorry," said Binny, looking apologetically at his stepmother, whose allergy to dogs and cats was so severe it could stop her breathing. "I didn't mean to bring him in. I just ran without thinking."

"Why?" asked Gareth.

Binny's eyes spoke for her, *I'll tell you later,* so plainly that Gareth's stepmother laughed.

"We were just going out," she told Binny. "We'll leave you and Gareth to talk in peace. Come on, come on!"

she added, pushing her husband toward the door. "Eat up the shortbread, you two, and anything else you like!"

"Great!" said Gareth, the moment the front door closed. "I've been wanting the place to myself! I want to see how much the pigeon can fly and I can't risk it outside till I know. Wait while I fetch it, then you can tell me what's the matter."

"It was the way she said it. 'I'm going to have to hurry you.' So quietly. So . . . so . . . knowingly. I can't explain."

Binny became silent. The pigeon, released from its cage, stretched its wings, one, then the other.

"Okay, you're right," said Gareth, at last. "You were right all along. She guesses you took that money; she's pretty sure she knows. I don't believe in witches but I bet she does and I bet she'd like to be one! I'm fed up with her anyway. She's asked my dad to stop me encouraging the local pigeons with food."

"Did she? Why? What did he say?"

"He said he'd make it a priority but he winked at me while he said it."

"She must have crept up behind me out there; that's why I jumped so much. What do you think she means, she's going to have to hurry me?"

"She's giving you a day or two more before she tells," said Gareth. "Come with me, while I think."

He picked up the pigeon (transformed in less than twenty-four hours from a bundle of grubby feathers to a white bird that might fly) and carried it into the hallway.

"Don't move," he told Binny, then dropped yellow seed on the hall floor and lifted the pigeon and set it on the bottom stair. He and Binny watched while it considered the seed, angling its head, one way and then the other.

"Go for it!" encouraged Gareth, and as if the pigeon understood, it scrambled clumsily for a moment and then fluttered down.

"It used both wings, did you see?" asked Gareth, triumphantly.

"Yes. Both wings. Why doesn't she tell now?"

"Because she can't go witching up to your mum saying, 'Saw Binny steal a pile of money,' without being sure. Not if she wants to stay speaking to her. Which she does, because she's after your house."

Binny looked mutinous. Gareth picked up the pigeon so quietly that it hardly stirred in his hand, dropped more seed, an irresistible amount, replaced the pigeon on the stair, and hung like a hawk above it while it flew and then pecked and gulped.

"I'll try it from the second stair next," he said, recapturing it, and then looked up at Binny's waiting face and asked, "What's the matter?"

"Where would we live if we sold the house?"

"In another one of course. Bigger. Bet your mum would be pleased."

"She *likes* sleeping on the sofa!"

"Yeah right," said Gareth.

The pigeon flew from two stairs, and then took a practice flight of its own, into the sitting room and across to the sofa.

"I've got to find that money," said Binny desperately. "Gareth, please help me. I can't bear Clem to have taken it. Or Pete."

"James!" said Gareth. "I don't know how I've forgotten to tell you about James. And have you seen Dill lately?"

"No."

"It's worth a look, if he's still at it. We can cross James off the list anyway now. I should have told you before. I don't know what he buried but it was something of Dill's, and Dill's furious."

"I never thought it was James," said Binny, loyally. "But what about Dill? He was round at our house every day until they quarreled. What did Dill bury?"

"James won't say. He's not supposed to know, but I think he does. Come on. We'll go and drag it out of him. I'll just put the pigeon back outside."

To be doing something made Binny feel better. They inspected Dill, still glaring out of his grandmother's window, and then went to look for James.

"I bet he's still behind the sofa," said Gareth, and he was, although now it was less of a refuge and more of a very comfortable cave, padded with cushions, decorated with daffodils and with a furtive view of the window so that he could watch for enemy attack. He lay amongst the cushions, drinking orange juice from a carton, and playing a Space Invaders game on Clem's phone.

"She said I could," he said, "to cheer me up. And Pete got me the daffodils . . ."

Binny averted her eyes from her mother's squashy green bag, still on its chair, and said, "Lovely."

"And I borrowed your quilt, Binny, in case I got cold, and I'm going to live behind here all day and go out and see my chickens at night when Dill'll be in bed. So do you think that'll be all right?"

In the dim light of the sofa cave his eyes looked dark and full of questions. He had done his best to make himself feel safe, but despite his cushions and daffodils, Binny could see that he was unhappy. Little James, still only six, she thought, and got down on her knees to comfort him.

"Don't kiss me!" said James, retreating hastily.

"You've stopped saying that," Binny reminded him. "James, Gareth told me a bit of what happened. Couldn't you just say that you're sorry you buried Dill's whatever-it-was, and you'll help him dig it up?"

"No."

"Why not? You are, aren't you?"

"It's no good if I am because I can't help dig it up. I didn't make a map so I don't know where it is."

"But Dill made a map, didn't he? That's what you

told Gareth. Wouldn't Dill's map help you?"

"Binny!" said James impatiently. "You don't under-stand about treasure burying! Dill buried his in one place. I buried mine in another place with a feather stuck on top. Dill didn't put my feather on his map. He only put his coffee tin of money."

Binny suddenly clutched Gareth's arm very tightly.

"Dill's coffee tin had money in it?" asked Gareth, as casually as he could.

"Yes'n bare ladies on the outside. Gold bare ladies," said James, "with very long hair. Everything is boring without Dill."

Gareth took charge. He unclamped Binny's fingers, dismissed the gold bare ladies with a wave of his hand, and became stern. "How d'you know about the money in Dill's tin?" he demanded. "I thought you said it was a secret what he buried."

"It is, but I heard when he made his map," said James. "That's how I know. He leaned on a rock to write and he spelled it to himself out loud: '*m-u-n-n-y.*' Like that."

Binny found herself suddenly trembly with relief. The money was safe. Not fallen irrevocably through the space between worlds. Not seized by Clem, rest-less, secretive, short tempered, and guilty though her sister seemed these days. Not filched by Pete. (Dismiss, then, from thought, the image of Pete, her mother's bag in his large builder's hands.) Nor had it been taken by anyone else. It had simply been lost in a game, by two very small boys, so little that they couldn't even be counted as guilty.

"Binny!" said Gareth, interrupting these thoughts. "Binny, wake up!"

"What?"

"I'm going with James to see if he can talk to Dill . . . Shut up, James, don't argue!"

"He might kung fu me," said James.

"You'll have to risk it," said Gareth. "You want to be friends again, don't you? Go and get your shoes and be fast!"

"I've just got used to living in my cave."

"No you haven't. You said everything was boring without Dill."

"Well it is."

"Come on, then!"

"I've got to tell Clem or Pete if I go out."

"So do it. Quick!"

"If Dill starts kung fu-ing me will you and Binny grab him?"

"Definitely."

"I'll come, then," said James, crawling out of his cave. "I'll tell Clem and Pete now."

"We've found it!" said Binny, as soon as he was out of the way. "Gareth! Gareth! We've found it! We just need that map."

"Soon as we get Dill out of his house we'll find a way

to get it," said Gareth. "Then we'll just have to hope the tin's still there."

"It's only been two days and there's hardly anyone on the beaches."

"As long as they buried it above the high tide mark," said Gareth, but that was such an unbearable thought that Binny could not even consider it.

"Let's go and get Dill," she said, and led the way to the door.

Getting Dill was not a simple thing to do. James waved and signaled hopefully, but it was not enough. Dill, like other superpowers, preferred menace to negotiation, and it took a force from within to get him out into the street.

The force from within was Dill's grandmother, angry at the loss of her ancient coffee tin, harassed by the need to explain her grandson's window performances to passersby, and absolutely tired of having him under her feet all day. Dill's grandmother was a superpower herself. When she saw James waving and beckoning in the street she picked up Dill under one arm, like a person might pick up a plank or a roll of carpet, and dumped him onto the doorstep.

"And mind," she told him fiercely before she banged shut the door, "you stay away from that beach!"

On the doorstep Dill subsided, toes crossed, arms wrapped around his legs, his chin on his bony knees, and his eyes tight shut. He did not look dangerous. James inched closer and closer and at last, very cautiously, sat down beside him.

"Dill," he said.

Dill unwrapped his arms from his legs, pushed his fingers in his ears, and continued sulking.

Nothing happened for what seemed like a long time. James became cold and Binny went back to the house to fetch him a jacket. Gareth began to sort through the collection of beach junk that had accumulated in his pockets. A plastic fork, some bottle tops, a baby's pale blue sock. A black Lego dragon, waterworn and dull. A pen, a cigarette lighter, and a key ring with a one legged Spider-Man attached. Gareth tried the pen, flicked the cigarette lighter, balanced the dragon on his hand, and dangled Spider-Man by his chain.

James erupted from the doorstep.

He grabbed Spider-Man. He ran around in a circle. He jumped up and down, hugging himself. He shouted, "Look! Look! Look! Look! Look!"

Dill remained as unmoved as a limpet on a rock.

James set to work on him. He unclamped his chin from his knees, pulled his fingers from his ears, and pried open an eye. He pushed Spider-Man into his face, and he said, "Look, look, look, look! Spider-Man! Look!"

Then at last Dill looked, and after one cnormous shout of "SPIDER-MAN!" lunged, grabbed, and then seemed to go into a trance.

"What's happening?" asked Binny, back with James's jacket.

"It's his Spider-Man!" explained James, all radiant as a dandelion flower. "Dill's Spider-Man! His Spider-Man key ring!"

"So what?"

"The Spider-Man key ring that he dropped and I buried. That I buried and was lost and I only put a feather. How did you know where to dig?"

Gareth said he hadn't dug, he hadn't had to, the key ring had not been buried and that he'd found it when he was picking up junk.

"Junk!" said James, aghast. "Junk! Did you hear that, Dill? He just called your Spider-Man junk!"

"Well," said Gareth, "he's broken. He's only got one leg."

"He's got *two* legs," said Dill, coming suddenly to life. "Two legs but one's come *off*."

"It's stuck in a keyhole," said James. "In his gran's little cupboard keyhole because she always keeps it locked. Dill told me."

"That doesn't mean he hasn't got two legs," said Dill.

"One here, one there," agreed James.

"If you didn't dig him up," said Dill, looking suspiciously at Gareth, "how did he get unburied?"

"Sand moves all the time," said Gareth. "Gets blown about. Gets kicked up. Nothing's going to stay buried in sand for long."

"Isn't it?"

"Not unless it's very deep."

"How deep?" asked Dill. "Deeper'n that?"

He held his hand at about knee height from the pavement to show how deep he meant.

"Ha!" said Gareth. "Just a bit!" And he tried not to look triumphant at the new expression on Dill's face, which was the worried look of someone who wishes they had not buried their gran's special coffee tin with real money inside, in a few centimeters of soft shifting sand.

James saw Dill's face too, and understood his thoughts.

"Dig it up," he said. "You've got a map."

Dill looked nervously over his shoulder at his gran's closed door.

"You're seven!" said James.

Dill acknowledged this with a downward smile.

"Gareth'll go with you," said James. "Won't you Gareth?"

The moment was coming that Gareth had been working for.

"Why not?" he asked.

Dill looked again at his gran's front door and shook his head.

"Go for you, then, if you like," said Gareth, and he spoke as casually as if he couldn't care less if Dill agreed or not.

"With the map?" asked Dill.

"Yeah, all right," said Gareth.

"Promise you won't open it without me?"

"Promise," said Gareth.

Chapter Fifteen

✳ ✳ ✳

Later on Wednesday Afternoon

Binny and Gareth and Max set off for the beach. James and Dill were left behind. They didn't care. They were as passionately friends as they had been enemies an hour before. Dill offered James a shared ownership of Spider-Man. James offered Dill the best cushion in his cave. Binny and Gareth abandoned them with thankfulness.

"Map," said Gareth when they reached the sands, and they bent to look at it.

"It's not a map at all!" said Binny after staring for a moment.

On the paper that Dill had given Gareth was a picture of the top half of a large thin lady with no clothes on. As far as Binny could see, it gave no clue as to where any treasure hunt should begin.

However, Gareth was more hopeful. "It must be near where I found that key ring," he said, grinning at Dill's illustration.

"Could you find the place again?"

"Think so. Come on."

They ran, and Max ran with them, until the town beach was left behind. "Slow down now," ordered Gareth, pausing to look around. "It might have been somewhere about here."

Once more they got out Dill's map. The bare lady seemed as enigmatic as ever to Binny's eyes, but Gareth saw more. "Look!" he said, pointing. "That's James!"

James, rather squashed on the edge of the paper and identifiable only by his hat, leaned against a triangular rock, some distance from the bare lady. She, when Binny looked closer, seemed to be surrounded by a garland of sharks' teeth. MUNNY spelled letters in one corner of the paper, and a wavy line pointed over sand and rocks to the bare lady's stomach.

Gareth proceeded to translate all this with a briskness that stunned Binny. The bare lady was clearly the coffee tin, placed in the center of a ring of rocks, slightly to the left of a large and solitary boulder, and while Binny was still marveling at this braininess, Gareth had located not only the rock ring and the boulder, but also marked a circle in the sand around the place where they should dig.

"How stupid were we, though," he exclaimed at this point, "not to bring a spade!"

Not having a spade was made much better by the fact that they did have Max. When they realized what an efficient digger Max was they divided the circle into sections and got down to serious work.

It was not easy, but sometime in between Gareth remarking that they should have brought a metal detector, and Binny giving up hope entirely, a corner of red paint emerged.

"We've found it, we've found it, we've found it!" rejoiced Binny, and they had. There was Dill's coffee tin, bright red and gold. There were his bare ladies with their thoughtfully arranged hair. And whatever was inside moved when the tin was shaken with a dull and papery thump, exactly as a roll of slightly dampened twenty-pound notes might be expected to move.

"Promise you won't open it without me," Dill had said. Gareth had promised, but Binny hadn't, so they fought about it all the way home.

"*There* you are!" exclaimed Gareth's father, looming suddenly out of the shadows of Gareth's front door. "*At* last! Oh, no you don't! Don't even think of dodging round next door to hide! We leave you alone for half an hour and come back to find the entire

house waist deep in birdseed and (excuse my language Binny) PIGEON SHIT! I have been waiting here CURSING this past hour and I am absolutely damned if you get past me now! DON'T roll your eyes at me! IN! And clear up! As in, clear up to my admittedly OCD standards of immaculate hygiene, or else the ruddy pigeon goes! NOT you please, Binny."

It was amazing. It was awful. One minute the money was within moments of recovery. The next it was behind a closed door.

"Please, please!" Binny called, hammering very hard on that door with both fists and it opened very suddenly to reveal Gareth's six foot four inches, rugby scrumming, golf ball whacking, triathlon stampeding, iron willed, reckless tempered, unreasonable perfectionist relation filling every possible inch of the doorframe.

"*Not* today, thank you, Binny!" he said. "*Off* you pop! *Good*-bye!" And then the door was closed again, very firmly indeed.

"It's not fair!" she howled through the letterbox, but it remained shut and a movement from behind Miss Piper's lacy curtains sent Binny home again.

Back in her own home, things had become equally tense. As soon as Binny opened the door she felt it, like thunder in the air. She stood still at the foot of the stairs, her senses twitching with alarm as they searched for the source of the trouble.

Not James and Dill. She could hear their voices from

behind the living room sofa, the comfortable drone of two people talking at once and not listening to each other.

Not Clem. Her coat and bag were both gone from her peg by the kitchen door.

Memory echoed in the electric air. What was it, what was it, what was it, wondered Binny, and then suddenly she knew. It was an argument between two adults.

It was a strange, long forgotten feeling to Binny; the tension between rooms, the deadened weight of words unspoken. It startled her with its familiarity. For years and years she had remembered the time when her father was alive as one of steady perfection. Had there been arguments then? It seemed there must have been, because the echoes of memory suddenly found words:

Isn't that an awful lot to pay for a flute for a child?
and

You used to love adventures! When did that change?
and

A sheepdog puppy? Tell me you're joking!

At the time, these darknesses had hardly been noticed by Binny; they were grown-up clouds, and between them and behind them was always the steady summery brightness of the everyday world.

But Binny had grown older and she noticed the darkness now.

Suddenly voices came from the kitchen:

I trusted you!

It was nothing! Next to nothing!

Not next to nothing to me! I'd never have agreed if I'd known.

"Hello! Hello!" called Binny, appalled at finding herself eavesdropping. "Hello Mum, I'm here!"

There was no reply; they had not heard. Binny knocked on the door and then pushed it open just as Pete came storming out. His voice was very loud, "ALL RIGHT I THINK I'VE GOT THE MESSAGE. I'M OFF. Hey! What are you doing here?"

"I just . . . ," began Binny, but Pete was already thundering up the stairs and he did not stop to hear her reply.

"Binny!" called her mother from the kitchen.

"Oh hello!" said Binny, pink with guilt. "I just came in. I thought you would still be at work."

"Yes, so did Pete," said her mother grimly, ramming a saucepan into the cupboard as she spoke.

"Is everything all right?"

Binny's mother banged shut the cupboard door, leaned back against the kitchen wall, closed her eyes, and did the special counting-breathing that she herself had taught Binny to use in times of nightmare, panic, outrage, or great temper tantrums.

After at least a minute of this, she said, "Yes."

"Oh good. Is Pete . . ."

Binny stopped speaking and waited while her mother breathed deeply in on a count of seven, and slowly out again, on a count of eleven. Clearly she did not want to talk about Pete.

"I'll make you a cup of tea," Binny offered.

"I DON'T WANT . . . ," began Binny's mother (from whom Binny had undoubtably inherited her own terrible temper) and then began counting again.

Up to seven, down to eleven.

"Thank you Binny. That would be nice."

"Open your eyes," suggested Binny.

Her mother did this and said peacefully, "Just a misunderstanding. Nothing for you to worry about."

"Everyone is screaming and swearing today," said Binny, knowing from experience how comforting it is to hear about other people's temper failures when you are having to endure your own. "You should have heard Gareth's dad just before I came in. Worse than you. Horrible. About nothing. Well, hardly anything. Here's your tea."

"I wasn't screaming and swearing."

"'Course you weren't," said Binny, patting her arm.

A tremendous thudding now began on the stairs, Pete, weighed down by two enormous tool bags, one over each shoulder.

"Would you like a cup of tea too?" Binny asked him, feeling very much the grown-up amongst all the bangs and flashes.

"NO I SOMETHING-WELL WOULDN'T THANK YOU," said Pete very forcefully. "I'm finished here."

Then to Binny's astonishment he stumped through the living room, retrieved his spirit level from the mantelpiece, stuck it in his jacket pocket, and marched (slightly a staggering march because of the weight of the tool bags) out of the door.

Behind the sofa, James rolled his eyes, a new trick which he was mastering rather well. "Grown-ups!" he said to Dill. "Always in moods."

Dill nodded very primly, looking rather like his gran.

Binny did not understand what had happened, but she could not let Pete leave like that, not after all the time he had been with them.

"Wait!" she called, and ran down the street after him.

He didn't hear her. He was unlocking the doors of his old white van.

Thwack! that was the first tool bag dumped inside.

Bang! that was the second.

Pete straightened his shoulders, slammed shut the doors, and pulled the spirit level out of his pocket. With it came a fragment of bubble wrap that opened and sparkled as it fell.

Clem's bracelet, the silvery moon, the flute, the curling treble clef, spilled from the wrapping onto the road. Pete stooped to pick it up just as Binny arrived beside him.

"Pete!" she exclaimed.

Pete's eyes looked coldly down at her.

"Clem's bracelet!"

"Yes," he said, and tipped it from his hand into her own.

"You'd better give it back," he told her. "Give it straight to Clem. And don't tell Pol . . ." He paused, and started again. "Don't tell your mother."

"Why not?"

"Not your business."

Binny clutched the bracelet tightly, her thoughts all whirling in her head and she had to swallow hard before she managed to ask, "Did Clem drop it?"

"She left it somewhere. I picked it up to keep it safe."

"Where?"

"Never you mind."

"You've packed up all your things."

"I have," said Pete, and shouldered his way past her, pulled open the driver's door, started the engine, and then leaned out of the window.

"You'd better look in the attic," he said.

"Look in the attic?"

"That's what I said," said Pete, and drove off leaving her still staring.

"He's gone!" said Binny to her mother. "How can he be gone? What happened? Why have I got to look in the attic?"

"Go and see," said her mother, as if relieved to have a reason to shoo Binny out of the kitchen. "Go on! It's a surprise, although how you haven't noticed yet is beyond me! I suppose you had Max and Gareth to keep you busy. Take Max! He can manage the stairs."

There were now stairs up to the attic. The old open

staircase Pete had brought to the garden, painted
blue, with a handrail, fixed neatly to the wall. Max
managed them in two bounds with Binny close behind
him.

She looked into the place that Pete had made. For
the family junk, he had said once, or perhaps the family
treasure.

There were blue wooden railings round the top of
the stairs with a little gate in them that opened into a
new white room, tent shaped, bright. It was hardly fur-
nished, but Binny's chest of drawers had been carried
up, and her bed was there too, waiting to be made, with
Max's basket beside it. There were other things too, but
Binny hardly saw them, because under the roof window that filled the room with light, was something so
astonishing it stopped her breath.

Her father's desk.

"How? How? How?" demanded Binny, turning round
to find her mother had followed her up the stairs. "How
is it there? Is it true? Is it staying? How?"

"Well, he fetched it. Pete. Pete fetched it out of storage in his van. For a surprise. He took the top off to
get it up, and then put it together again. What do you
think?"

"I don't know."

"You don't *know*?"

Binny knew she was being disappointing. She knew
she should be jumping around in joy, or crying tears

of memory, or asking a dozen questions. She should be hugging her mother (she did do that) and making her bed and admiring the skylight view and racing up and down the new staircase. But instead she simply stood.

"I can't think," she said.

Her brain needed untangling. Her father's desk. Clem's bracelet. Pete gone, and the tension in the air. The movement behind Miss Piper's curtains. James and Dill and their buried treasure. Gareth, and his stubborn belief in one world only, containing many lovely animals, infinite faulty humans, and no gaps.

"'Thank you' is a good word," said Binny's mother, opened the small blue gate, and stamped down the stairs.

"Thank you, thank you, thank you!" cried Binny, too late.

"Give it to us! Give it to us! Give me my tin!"

There was banging on the front door and it was Gareth. He was bumping it with his head while he fended off James and Dill with his arms. When Binny pulled it open they all fell through together in a grabbing, squabbling heap.

"Rugby scrums OUTSIDE!" ordered Binny's mother, appearing before them in her worst temper in years, and rushed the whole lot through the kitchen and into the back garden.

In the damp space behind the trash can they

untangled themselves. Gareth produced the coffee tin then, and held it high above his head.

"Give it!" demanded Dill. "You'd better not have opened it! Let me see!"

"Don't let him run off with it," said Binny urgently to Gareth. "Make him open it here."

"I mightn't want to!" growled Dill.

"You've got to," said Binny. "We know what's inside!"

"You don't!" Dill grabbed again as Gareth held it out of reach. "How do you know?"

"Worked it out," said Gareth. "We know it's money and we know it's not yours."

All the fight went out of Dill and he sagged against the trash can. James reached out a kind arm to his friend and even Binny spared him a glance, although her eyes were on Gareth, unpeeling the tape that Dill had wound round and round the lid.

"My treasure," moaned Dill.

"Let's face it, you stole it," said Gareth. "This needs scissors or something."

"Give it to me," begged Binny.

Now that the hunt was finished a calmness had come over her. It was going to be all right. Miss Piper would stop her witching. Soon it would be possible to walk through the town without fear. The final piece of tape came loose.

"Got it!" said Gareth.

Binny pried off the lid and tipped out a bundle of

damp brown paper, also taped. "At last," she sighed. "My money."

"S'not your money," said Dill sulkily.

"Sort of, it is. We've been looking for it all week."

"S'James's."

"What?"

"S'James's money."

"Mine!" cried James. "Mine! I haven't GOT any money! Show me!"

"Well, you needn't get mad," said Dill. "You buried my Spider-Man. I buried your money. Fair. Give it to me now."

He grabbed the bundle from Binny, gnawed through the tape with his teeth, and scuffled through the wrappings. Then, before Binny's horrified eyes, he shook out two brown pennies.

"My PLAYGROUND pennies!" shrieked James in delight.

Gareth stood like a person stunned. James and Dill leaped in celebratory kung fu poses all around the trash can. Binny seized the red coffee tin with its glassily smiling bare ladies, emptied it out, and checked every scrap of tape-tangled wrapping paper, before staring wildly round the garden as if a fist full of twenty-pound notes might have blown away unnoticed.

Chapter Sixteen

✳ ✳ ✳

Wednesday Night and Thursday Morning

James was happy that night. He lay in bed, his small brown wooden boat of a bed, and gloated. He was back on the exciting, choppy seas of friendship with Dill. True, he had nearly capsized once or twice. He shouldn't have drawn black clothes on the coffee tin ladies. He shouldn't have confided to Dill that he had thought of killing him dead with a Star Wars lightsaber. Those had been difficult moments. But he had steered into safer water when he had given Dill one of his playground brown pennies. Dill had been so overwhelmed that he had promised to ask if James could visit him, next time his gran calmed down.

"Does she calm down much?" James had asked,

because secretly he would have preferred to visit on an uncalm day.

"No," Dill had replied, "not much. Not for very long either." Then he had looked thoughtfully at the red coffee tin. James had dressed the gold ladies with black felt pen and it hadn't cleaned off very well. They would never be as bare again, thought Dill regretfully, and he decided Dead Granddad's calendar would have to remain unshared until his friend was much older.

Still, Dill had hoped that James could visit soon. James had good ideas. "At your house," he had said, "we can do kung fu fighting shows in the window. It'll be better with two of us. And on the street outside we'll put a box with a notice. PAY HERE NOW. What'll we buy with the money?"

A tent and an Xbox, some chickens for Dill, two surfboards, and a drum kit.

"In the morning," said James, and sailed happily to sleep.

No one else was happy. Clem, Binny, and their mother were so separately miserable that they had not been kind to each other. James had produced Miss Piper's small white van before he went to bed.

"She gave it to me for a present," he had told Binny. "I asked if she didn't want it but she said not anymore."

"She's witched Pete away," said Binny. "That's why."

"For GOODNESS' SAKE Binny!" her mother had exclaimed, and later Binny heard her say to Clare's mum during a long and grumpy phone call, "Sometimes I feel like packing up and moving a hundred miles away!"

"When are you going to get your junk up into the attic?" Clem asked Binny. "Then Mum can have your room and stop sleeping on the sofa at last."

"I never thought of that," said Binny, and spent the rest of the evening climbing up and down her new staircase with her arms full of possessions. It took a very long time because as she packed she searched once again for the twenty-pound notes. By bedtime the attic, which had looked very large when she first saw it, had shrunk to a normal sized room, and her old bedroom, which had seemed very small, had expanded in every direction. Gareth, who came to say good night to Max and stayed to help carry things, was very rude about Binny's possessions.

"Teddy bears and stuff!" he said in disgust.

"Some are Clem's that I had to rescue when she threw them away."

"*Rescue!*"

"Their faces," explained Binny. "Their eyes . . ." She stopped. Useless to try and explain the pathos of an about-to-be-chucked-out teddy bear's eyes to Gareth. "Anyway, I like them, and I haven't rescued many of Clem's things. Just the bears and the dolls' house."

"Dolls' house?" asked Gareth. "Where?"

"Somewhere about."

Gareth was looking around the attic more carefully. "It's really good up here," he said. "Can you open up that skylight or is it fixed shut?"

It slid open easily. Binny climbed on her father's desk, and Gareth stood on the bedroom chair, and together they gazed at the night view of the town. Far away, a lighthouse flashed and paused and flashed again. Close by, Miss Piper's broomstick made a long shadow against her garden wall. In the eaves, feathery bundles of pigeons roosted, waiting for the next free meal to appear in Gareth's garden.

"She wouldn't be pleased if she knew they were there," said Gareth, glancing at the broomstick.

"Gareth, what'll I do?"

"It's Pete or Clem," he said.

But in bed that night Binny remembered Gareth's casual question: "*Dolls' house? Where?*"

Where was the dolls' house?

The dolls' house, with its miniature cupboards and wardrobes, held half a dozen hiding places, and Binny fell asleep recalling them, instead of the way Clem's eyes had looked when she had said of the broken flute: "It's paid for already."

Instead of remembering Pete, with the squashy green bag in his hand, and his cold eyes as the bracelet fell to the ground.

Instead of imagining Miss Piper's lapping voice saying to her money-hunted mother, *There's something I have to tell you about Binny.*

When Gareth arrived in the morning for Max's early walk there was one thought in Binny's mind.

"I need to find the dolls' house. It's lost."

"Lost? How can you lose a dolls' house? What's it like anyway? Does it open up or something? Surely you'd remember if you put money inside a dolls' house!"

"Would I?"

"'Course you would. What a weird thing to do."

"No it's not. I could easily have put it there. I often used to put things in it, just to tidy them away. I don't know where it is now, though. I gave it to James, but he didn't want it and it's not in his room. Nor in mine either, and I can't see it downstairs."

"What about Clem's room?"

"She's gone out. She rushed out early. I'll check, just in case."

It wasn't in Clem's room. It wasn't in the cupboard under the stairs either.

"Come out of there!" ordered Binny's mother crossly, as usual in a rush.

"I was just looking for the dolls' house," said Binny meekly.

"The dolls' house? What for? You were trying to give it to James not long ago. You shouldn't have; he dropped it down the stairs and the chimneys broke. It's being glued back together, I believe, so you'll have to wait till it's fixed."

"Has Pete taken it, then?" asked Binny, very surprised.

"Not Pete. Miss Piper."

"*Miss Piper?*"

"She offered," said Binny's mother, and disappeared into the bathroom.

"My whole life is going wrong!" wailed Binny, when she had gone. "What if the money's in there and Miss Piper finds it? We've got to get it back quick. Gareth . . ."

"No!" said Gareth at once. "I've had enough run-ins with that old bat! No way am I going with you while you ask, 'Please can I have my dolls' house back!' And to make quite sure this didn't happen he went off with Max, leaving Binny hovering outside Miss Piper's windows, gathering her courage.

The house seemed empty. No shadowy movements behind the lace curtains and silk flowers. No answer to Binny's knock on the door.

"I expect she's in town somewhere," said Binny's mother, pausing on her way to work with James in tow. "I'm taking James with me, and Clem should be back soon. There's cheese and apples and potato chips for sandwiches at lunchtime, or you can have a go at cooking if you're feeling enterprising."

"I don't think I will be."

"Well, perhaps Clem might. And don't go bothering Miss Piper for that dolls' house if she hasn't got it finished. I can't think what you want it for anyway."

"I just wanted to look inside very quickly."

"Gareth's not thinking of turning it into a pigeon coop or anything?"

"No, no! Of course not!"

"Be good then, Binny. I'll be back as soon as I can."

Binny was still being good outside Miss Piper's when she spotted Clem.

Clem, half running, half stumbling up the steep cobbled street from the market, her head held down to hide her face. She passed Binny without seeming to see her at all, tripped over the doorstep, flung herself through the front door, and went racing up the stairs.

Even from the street outside, Binny could hear the sobs.

"Clem?" she called, running after her. "Clem?"

"Leave me ALONE!"

"Has something awful happened?"

Sob, went Clem.

"Shall I ring Mum at work?"

"Don't you dare!"

Clem appeared then at her bedroom door, blotchy faced, mascara streaked eyes, messy haired, such an achingly younger version of her usual self, that Binny reached out and hugged her.

"Oh Clem!"

"Shut up, shut up, shut up," moaned Clem, slumping back onto her bed. "Don't tell Mum. Don't tell anyone. Don't look at me like that!"

"What's happened?"

"I've done something awful."

"No Clem, you can't have. Not awful. Not you."

"I didn't want to," said Clem, with her head in her arms.

"Of course you didn't." Binny patted a quivering shoulder with such sympathy that for a moment Clem stopped sobbing.

Only for a moment, though, then her body began to shake again and she said, "You would never understand."

"I might," said Binny humbly. "I've done loads of awful things myself."

"Well, you're used to it," sniffed Clem. "You should be anyway," she added so callously that Binny would have marched out of the room if she had not had to ask: "Did you . . . did you . . . take something, Clem?"

"What do you mean, take something? Steal something? Is that what you mean?"

"Money," said Binny, hating what she was doing, but doing it anyway. "You didn't take a whole lot of money did you? Twenty-pound notes . . ." Binny's voice trailed away at the sight of the bewilderment on her sister's face. "No," she said. "No you didn't."

"Are you mad, Binny? Whatever could make you ask that? Twenty-pound notes? I wish!"

"I knew you wouldn't have."

"I would!" said Clem. "I would if I could! It would have been better."

"Better than what?"

"I can't tell you. You'd hate me. Please shut up now Binny and leave me alone. I just want to be miserable for a bit."

"I was only trying to help."

"I know."

"Would you like a cup of tea?"

"No thank you. Haven't you got anything to do?"

"Millions of things."

"Go and do them, then."

"The first is Miss Piper. I've got to get the dolls' house off her. She's mending it or something."

"Who cares?"

"Oh."

"What do you want it for, anyway?"

"I just do. But it's going to be awful. Oh Clem, stop crying!"

"Sorry, sorry, sorry. Please just leave me alone, Bin."

"All right. Oh. I forgot. Your bracelet. Here."

"WHAT!"

The restoration of Spider-Man to Dill was nothing compared to the return of the bracelet to Clem.

Clem stared, seized, stared again, and then all at once began to cry in frightening, anguished howls, *Hooo, hooo, hooo,* the way no one in the family had cried for years and years. The way Clem had cried when her father had died.

"Clem! Stop it! Stop it!" begged Binny. "Someone will hear! Gareth's family! Miss Piper! Clem, I really will have to ring Mum!"

"Hooo!" wailed Clem one last time, and then as suddenly as she had started, she stopped, rocked for a little, and then said, in a fairly normal voice, "I thought I'd never see it again! How did you get my bracelet?"

"You must have dropped it," said Binny.

"What?"

Binny was suddenly very uncomfortable. As far as she knew, Pete had only ever been kind. Grumpy some-times, but kind. And she liked him very much. Yet too well she remembered the green bag and the bracelet falling, Miss Piper's hints.

All her money, gone missing . . .

Clem was insisting. "I didn't drop it. I knew where it was. Tell me how you got it."

"Someone gave it to me to give to you," said Binny reluctantly.

"Who? Mum?"

Binny shook her head.

"Please tell me?"

"Please don't make me. Why did you think you'd never see it again?"

"I sold it."

"Sold it?" asked Binny, truly shocked.

"Yes."

"Sold it to Pete?"

"To Pete? Of course not! I sold it to a jewelers' shop in town."

"Well then," said Binny, helplessly. "Well then, I don't understand."

"Listen," said Clem, and explained how her flute had been broken. "They should be serviced," she said, "like a car, but I could never afford it. So it had to be mended and I hadn't any money and the café was closed so I couldn't earn any."

"Hadn't you any saved up?"

Clem explained about the tremendous cost of flute lessons, and exam fees, and music books, and all the other things it took to study an instrument at such a high level, and also how she had nothing left to sell. Nothing at all.

"Except the bracelet. So I took it to that scuffy little jewelers' near the marketplace. The one with the notice saying 'Gold and silver bought.' They wouldn't buy it until I showed them my student ID card to prove I was old enough to let them and then they put it straight into the window for sale."

"I asked them not to," continued Clem. "I was so scared Mum would see it. There were cases inside the shop they could have put it in instead. At the beginning I thought maybe when I'd earned some money I could go back and buy it, but when I saw it in the window I knew I never could. They put the price underneath it. It was twice as much as they paid me. And when I went in and complained . . ."

"You didn't!" exclaimed Binny at this bravery.

"Of course I did. Dad's bracelet! I hated that man in the shop. He had a big white face and he smiled at me and said, 'This is a business, my dear.'"

"Cheating pig!" said Binny.

"Yes he was!"

"Is that why you've been so miserable? And in and out all the time?"

Clem nodded. "I kept checking it was still there. Every day, whenever I had a chance. And the last time I checked, just now, just half an hour ago, it was gone. Sold."

"Sold?"

"Yes. I asked, but they wouldn't tell me who bought it."

"It was Pete," said Binny. "It must have been. He gave it to me last night, just before he drove away."

"Pete did?"

"Yes. He said not to tell Mum but to say to you that he'd picked it up to keep it safe before it got lost. And he said I was to give it back to you."

"*It was more than a hundred pounds!*" said Clem.

"Those charms are white gold, not silver! That star is a diamond! How could Pete buy it?"

Binny did not want to think about how Pete could buy it. Instead she asked, "Was that the awful thing you did, selling your bracelet?"

"Yes."

"I did something much worse than that," said Binny, but Clem was turning and turning the bracelet on her wrist and she did not hear.

Chapter Seventeen

* * *

Thursday Afternoon
The Unbewitching

Clem had sold her bracelet, her last gift from her father and her most desperate selling yet. A year before, a month before, even a week before, Binny would have been furious and bewildered at such a betrayal, but not anymore. She understood about money now.

Poor Clem, she thought, and remembering how she had got it back again, *Oh Pete.*

Mostly however, Binny thought of the dolls' house. It had been in her room the night she lost the money. It still might save Pete. It still might save them both.

So once again she knocked on Miss Piper's door, and this time she knew that it would be opened. There was a light shining somewhere beyond the frosted glass panel, and soft movements behind the lace curtains. Binny chewed her nails and twisted her hair into worried knots and waited for the blue eyes and the lapping voice.

"Binny. You've come to see me at last."

"Yes," agreed Binny, and she nodded and nodded with nervousness. "Yes," she said again, and dried up.

"There's something you'd like to tell me?" suggested Miss Piper.

"To ask you," said Binny.

"Ask me?" The blue eyes became bright with surprise.

"Please could we have our dolls' house back?"

Miss Piper's whole shape changed. She stepped back and stared.

"Your dolls' house?" she repeated.

"Yes."

"You're here to ask for your dolls' house? That's all?"

"Yes please. Mum said you were mending it. Thank you very much, but I can mend it."

Miss Piper seemed unconvinced. "Why just now?"

"I didn't know it was here before," explained Binny. "I came as soon as Mum told me, but you were out."

"Well," said Miss Piper, "I thought you had come to see me on quite a different matter. And here's Clem too!"

A Clem transformed had arrived behind Binny,

not just her bracelet sparkling, but the whole of her sparkling with joy. "College rang! My flute is back! I'm just going to collect it!"

"It's been mended so soon?" asked Miss Piper, and Clem said, "Yes, so soon!" and didn't think to ask how she knew it had been broken.

"Please," said Binny desperately, "would you mind if Clem helped me carry my dolls' house back?"

"I would never have suspected you of caring about a dolls' house," said Miss Piper, and although she smiled and her voice was as smooth as ever, she looked at Clem as if asking a question.

Clem said, "Oh, yes, Binny does! She always did. That's why we've kept it so long," and Binny felt herself blushing at all the attention and scuffled a little with her feet.

"You'd better take it, then," said Miss Piper, moving aside. "It's in the sitting room, behind the door. I'm afraid I've hardly had time to look at it yet."

"Thank you," said Binny, and she was truly thankful for that news. "Thank you, thank you! Come on Clem!"

Miss Piper looked at them both curiously as they passed, so curiously that Clem paused to ask, "Miss Piper?"

"Nothing, nothing," said Miss Piper, waving them away, and she said something else that Binny did not catch.

"What was it?" she asked Clem, as they heaved the

dolls' house first up the main stairs and then up the attic stairs.

"She said, 'I may have been mistaken,'" said Clem as she dumped down her end of the burden. "What did she mean? Oh, it doesn't matter! Can you manage now? I'm going for my flute."

"Yes, go," said Binny, and even before Clem was down the attic stairs, she was on her knees in front of the dolls' house. She was very tired, as tired as a traveler at the end of a long journey. "Please," she whispered out loud, and undid the catch that opened it up.

The whole front swung open. Every room was visible, and Binny, who had forgotten until then the peg doll people, saw that every floor was inhabited. There was a small wooden Clem, four inches high, slumped across the sofa in the dolls' living room. No wonder she was slumped: her flute (a silver twirl of foil and wire) lay broken on the floor.

Upstairs, in the blue bedroom, a miniature James lay neatly in bed, tucked in immovably tight. His eyes gazed blankly at the ceiling above; he was clearly and firmly banished.

That's how she did it, thought Binny.

On the staircase between the floors sat Binny herself, her notebook fallen but her left hand still tight in her pocket, gripping the invisible money.

It was still invisible.

Binny searched under beds and inside cupboards,

but there was no money there. The dolls' house did not have an attic but she remembered the space under the roof. It held nothing but dust and the batteries for the fairy lights that long ago, in a different world, her father had strung through the house to surprise them all.

Binny remembered his voice, "Push that switch!"

She pushed it again, and jumped in surprise as silvery light sprang through the shadowy rooms. James tumbled out of bed and Clem's flute suddenly sparkled, Binny-on-the-stairs turned a somersault and her hand fell out of her empty pocket, and Binny herself, Binny the traveler at the end of the journey, was unbewitched at last.

It was a strange, strange feeling, like waking after an endless, muddled dream. It took a long while to feel real.

An hour passed, and then another. Gareth returned with Max and went off again to donate his art installation to the gallery in town. Clem tracked down Pete. He was easy to find; he was outside the jeweler's shop, sandpapering the window frames.

"Oh Pete!"

"Didn't cost me a penny," said Pete.

"Thank you, thank you!"

"What's the fuss? You get your bracelet. They get a coat of paint. Everyone's happy."

"Are you?"

"Never been better," said Pete, and tried to whistle a bit to prove it.

James came home with his mother and then spent a very short time kung fu fighting in the window with Dill. Dill's grandmother was not at all calm about this, so James helped Dill pack to run away. "You can come to our house," he offered, but Dill had already decided on China and would not change his mind.

Binny's mother spent the afternoon throwing things away, which she liked to do in times of stress.

Gareth returned from the gallery a local celebrity, having been photographed three times, interviewed twice, and given his autograph to a seven-year-old girl.

"You found it!" he exclaimed, the moment he saw Binny. "Where was it? That dolls' house?"

"No it wasn't. I haven't. But Gareth, I know what to do!"

She was a different Binny, the struggle of bewitchment gone from her face, her eyes bright with plans.

"Listen Bin, I've been thinking," said Gareth. "You're the only person who ever actually saw that money. And you know what you're like! Are you sure you didn't dream it?"

"Of course I'm sure. I took it. I lost it. And tomorrow, as soon as the bank is open, I'm going to tell them everything."

"You're mad," said Gareth flatly.

"I'm not. I should have done that ages ago instead of blaming everyone else."

"It wasn't blaming them. It was checking them out. We're still not certain it wasn't Clem or Pete."

"I am. You will be when I tell you. Anyway, I know who it was. It was me."

"You took it, but then what? It didn't fall through a hole in the world! You can't tell that to the bank!"

Binny, who was now absolutely convinced that this was exactly what had happened, decided not to argue. Instead she said, "I'm going to tell them that I'll pay it back myself."

"Binny, think before you do anything daft," said Gareth. "Don't go hoping that the bank will let you off, because I bet they won't."

"I don't want to be let off."

"Nobody knows but me. Even if that old witch next door guesses something, she can't prove it or she would have done it by now. Why don't you just keep quiet and forget it?"

"Because I want to pay it all back."

"Oh come on, Bin!" exploded Gareth. "You don't even know how much it was."

"Perhaps the bank will know."

"And how will you pay it back?"

"I'll earn it," said Binny stubbornly.

"Earn it!" said Gareth.

"The café will reopen soon. I earned money last summer."

"Cleaning tables for tips!"

"Yes. And I can do other things too. I could babysit . . ."

"You!"

". . . and find a paper route. Clem had a paper route when she was the same age as me. I can work all summer."

"Are you going to tell anyone besides the bank about all this?"

"I might. I might even tell Miss Piper. I'm not scared of her anymore."

"She's not a witch, then, after all?" asked Gareth sarcastically, and was dragged up to Binny's attic to see the witching in the dolls' house, the bed-trapped James, the broken flute, and the unhappy model of herself.

"They're just dolls shoved in any old way like any nutter might do," said Gareth, but his voice was uncertain as he looked, and looked again.

"I think she can witch people," said Binny. "But the witching only lasts if they let her. James didn't let her. He bounced out of bed the next morning. Clem didn't either. She got her flute fixed. And I'm not going to let her anymore. That's why I'm going to tell before she does, as soon as the bank opens in morning."

"Perhaps you're right," said Gareth slowly.

"Of course I am."

"Tomorrow is Friday, don't forget, that's when we have to go."

"You'll be back for summer," said Binny bravely, with her arms around Max.

"I wish I could come to the bank with you, but we always set off so early."

"I'd rather go by myself. I can't wait to begin making everything back to how it was before. I wish there was something I could do to start it now. Oh! I've just thought! There is!"

"What's that?"

"I'm going to see Clare. She's back from that school trip today! I'm going there right now!"

Chapter Eighteen

* * *

Thursday Evening

It was a long walk out to Clare's house, across the marketplace and then along the only road out of town, an always-breezy highway that started off between stone houses and shops, passed through a dreary stage of gas stations and tattoo parlors, skirted the permanently half built sports center, and then suddenly acquired grassy verges and became a country road, complete with dandelions, car flung litter, squashed squirrels, and airy blue views of the moors on the horizon.

Somewhere far out on those moors a big cat roamed, a dusty bronze lynx with feather tufted ears. Binny knew it existed because she and Clare had put it there, one frightening and beautiful autumn dawn.

A long walk, Binny thought, remembering. "A journey," she told Max. "Longer than this. Colder too."

Max pushed his nose into her hand to show that he was listening. All along the road his tail had kept up a steady swing of pleasure; no walk was ever too long for Max, but at the turn into the narrow side road that led to Clare's house the swing became an exuberant wave, because coming toward them was Clare.

Will she be friends, Binny had wondered, all through the journey. One glance at Clare showed that she already was.

"Binny! Binny! Max!" she cried, and Max hurtled toward her with Binny towing behind him, so that they met breathless and laughing in the middle of the road.

"I was just thinking about you!" said Clare, untangling herself from Max's leash, "and there you were! We're not still enemies, are we? I don't think we should be; it gets boring so fast. Do you still think Mum and me stole your money?"

"I never did," said Binny. "I promise I never did. It was me."

"You stole your own money?"

"Not my own. Clare, I've had an awful week."

"You'd better tell me," said Clare.

"That's what I came to do. Listen!"

Then Binny paused for a long time, while Clare looked at her expectantly.

"I am listening," she said at last.

"I know. Wait."

There was another very long pause.

"I am waiting," said Clare.

"It's hard to think of the words to begin," said Binny apologetically.

Clare nodded.

"I'm thinking of them now."

"Okay."

"I may get things a bit wrong."

"Look, you don't have to tell me," said Clare. "Tell me something else instead. What happened to your hair?"

"That's part of it."

"Oh."

"Not the main part, though."

"Did you mean it to be that color?"

"It's fence color."

"Yes. Did you mean . . ."

"No. Forget my hair."

Clare, who had been leading the way back along the lane to her house, now took charge. "Sit here!" she ordered, steering Binny toward a battered wooden bench beside the front door. "Give me Max. Shut your eyes. It's easier to talk with your eyes shut."

Binny handed over Max's leash, shut her eyes, and found Clare was right. Words came at once.

"It started when I was walking home from school

last Friday and I hadn't hardly any money for Mum's
birthday."

"And you weren't going on the trip with us," suggested Clare.

"There were loads of things I wanted money for,"
admitted Binny. "The more I thought of them, the more
I wanted." She paused, remembering her shopping list
of presents. Clare stroked Max and waited until she
went on again, and reached the marketplace where
the pigeons were flying, and then arrived at the unat-
tended ATM. "And I picked it up," finished Binny. "It
felt like leaves. Dry leaves, in my pocket and I took it
home."

She stopped.

Clare said, "I'd have done just the same."

Binny's eyes flew open in astonishment.

"Would you? Would you?"

"All that money? Of course I would! Think what you
could do with it!"

"You can't do anything," said Binny. "I found that
out almost straightaway. And you have to keep hiding
it. I hid it so many times I lost it. All I wanted to do was
give it back, but I couldn't find it anywhere. So that's
why I asked you. I'm sorry."

"Doesn't matter. But what are you going to do now?"

"Pay it back," said Binny at once. "I'm going to
go to the bank tomorrow and tell them everything
that happened and then I'm going to save up and get

summer vacation jobs until I can pay it all back."

"I'll help you!" said Clare, immediately. "We'll get it in no time! How much was it anyway?"

"Too much to count."

"Wow!" said Clare. "Too much to count, just waiting to be collected! I'd definitely have taken it! Now, forget it for a bit and come into the house. I'll tell you about the trip and we'll get something to eat. There's chocolate brownies and leftover sausages. I can't stop being hungry. They starved us all week."

"Did you like it, though? Did you do all that stuff about finding who you really are?"

"Mmm," said Clare, making large sausage sandwiches. "Oh yes, we did all that. I've got amazing people skills and extraordinary tact but I'm still going to be an explorer."

"I suppose they'll come in useful," said Binny. "I wonder if I've got them too."

"No," said Clare very certainly. "You've got awful people skills. I've never known anyone worse at people than you!"

"What was that other thing you've got?"

"Tact."

Binny grinned, and thought how much she liked Clare, despite her people skills and tact, and also Clare's mother, who came in and hugged her as if she hadn't seen her for weeks, and even Clare's grown-up brother Mark, despite the fact that he had once nearly accidentally shot her, and ever since had treated her like an edge-of-extinction species, saying such things as "Stand away from the microwave, Bin," and handing her cushions and vitamin tablets. They all sat around the kitchen table watching Clare eat and listening to her complain.

"It was salad every meal and no proper puddings," she said, eating dry bread and sauce because the sausages had run out. "I'm never leaving home again without emergency supplies. Can I open a can of beans?"

Mark reached in a cupboard and found her a can. She ate them cold with a fork without bothering with a plate.

Binny asked, "What did you do, besides starve?"

"Oh," said Clare, not pausing in her scooping of beans. "Everything they told us we would. Caving, the caves smelled horrible, like dead sheep, there was a dead sheep . . ."

"In the cave?"

"Nearby. And rappelling (it was more waiting than rappelling I only got one turn) and we had to write a play about glue sniffing to put us off doing it if we were thinking of trying, but I don't think anyone was. It would have been better if it had been about getting drunk because three people smuggled in vodka in shower gel bottles and drank it on the first night. They were really sick. I don't think they'd rinsed all the shower gel out. Their parents got telephoned to fetch them home."

"You're making everything sound rubbish so I don't feel bad about missing it," said Binny.

"I'm not! Well, I am, but only partly."

"But did everyone find out what they were going to be?"

"Sort of. Not the alcoholics. But there was a computer program with trick questions and an obstacle course where you got points for cheating and they put the results together. That's how I found out about my people skills and tact. Binny, you can't go back to school with your hair looking like that!"

"Clare!" said her mother. "Don't be rude!"

"It's all right. I hate it too," said Binny. "But it washes out in twenty-four washes."

"Twenty-four?" asked Clare, and when she and Binny were alone in her bedroom, asked, "How many have you done?"

"Three."

"Come on, then," said Clare, and led her into the bathroom where she ordered her to hang her head over the edge of the bath. Twenty-one scrubs and rinses later, Binny half swam to her feet at last, and after a short hot session with Clare's hair dryer found she was almost back to her familiar seaweed color again.

"That's better," said Clare. "Mum said she'd drive

you home and I've brought you back a present. There wasn't much to choose from, but I thought you'd like a pen."

"A pen?"

"Because you're a writer."

A writer.

There was no time for writing when Binny got home. Clare's mother dropped her off, just in time to see Pete leaving. He had arrived with one of his familiar suggestions: "Just a thought . . ." And at those words Clem had seized James, pushed him into his coat and shoes, and hurried him out of the house.

"Where to?" James had asked.

"An adventure," Clem had told him firmly, and she had kept him out adventuring until the sea became shadowy and the sky turned dusky purple. She brought him back, stuffed full of hot doughnuts from the stall by the harbor, just as the first stars began to come out, a minute or two after Binny arrived with Max.

"You needn't have all disappeared," said the children's mother reproachfully, when she finally returned to the kitchen and found them all there.

"Oh yes we need," said Clem.

"But since you're here, all together, I wonder . . . I'd like to . . . I think it would help . . ."

"Get on with it, Mum," said Clem kindly.

"To have a quick chat!"

"About Miss Piper?" asked Binny, suddenly uneasy.

"No, no, no! About Pete."

"Pete?"

"Remember Pete?" asked her mother.

"Yes," said Clem. "We remember Pete. If you mean the Pete who has lived here on and off since last October. The one who whistles and digs the garden and makes you laugh and builds attics into bedrooms and stuffs money into people's bags when he thinks they won't notice."

"Does he?" asked Binny, very surprised, and then answered herself, "Yes he does! I've seen him!"

"And behind the clock," said James.

"Is that where it came from?" asked Clem.

James nodded. "Yes, I saw him. And he gets nits off chickens too. And did you know he can juggle?"

"Can he?" said Binny.

"Yes he can," the children's mother admitted. "He was juggling on the roof the first time I saw him."

"The roof is fixed on very tightly," said Binny. "Remember how I checked? And he had a huff afterward?"

"He has huffs," said James.

"Huffs, and he doesn't like being paid," said Clem.

"Short huffs, though," said Binny. "He huffs off, then he comes back with a new idea. I like it when he says, 'Just a thought . . .'"

"Then you know it will be something good," agreed James.

"Do you?" said his mother.

"Good, or really good, or even fantastic," said Binny, as bravely, and lovingly, and reassuringly as she could, and Clem and James nodded.

"Are you quite sure?" asked the children's mother.

"Yes," said Binny.

"Yes," said James.

"Of course," said Clem.

The whole of the rest of the evening, every single minute of it, was taken up with discussing Pete's latest idea. By the time Binny and Max went up to bed in the attic, the skylight was quite dark. Binny looked around the dim triangular room. The dolls' house stood in a corner. Clare's pen was on the desk. Max was curled in his basket.

Tomorrow he would be leaving with Gareth.

Oh! thought Binny, I wish I hadn't remembered that!

It took all her daylight bravery away, so that the night clouds in the skylight became mottled and fearful.

Tomorrow she would have to go to the bank.

Down and down and down fell Binny's courage, until an idea reached out like a friendly hand to save her.

Tomorrow, when it's all over, I will write it down.

Chapter Nineteen

* * *

Friday morning

Everyone understood that Binny was useless at good-byes, especially when it came to Max and Gareth. Once they were gone, back to Oxford where Max lived during term time with Gareth and his mother, then she was quite all right again. No one could take care of Max better than Gareth; Binny knew that. Also, he was just as much Gareth's dog as hers; if she had had him first, then Gareth had had him longest. It was all quite fair, and yet even so the partings were dreadful. Binny's unhappiness would chew like an ache, and she would find herself weeping for no good reason. It was very embarrassing and damp and it went on and on, all through the long, exhausting process of sorting and packing.

"What time are you leaving?" she asked Gareth, meeting him in the garden, early that Friday morning.

"Eight, he hopes. Eight thirty more like, she guesses."

"I'm going to stay out of the way. I can't bear all the fuss. I hate saying good-bye . . ."

"Me too . . ."

"So don't let's."

"Binny . . ."

It was happening already. Tears. Binny scrubbed at her eyes with her fists while Gareth searched for cheering remarks.

"You'll manage at the bank. You'll be fine. I was thinking about it. You're right. It is the thing to do."

"Yes."

"And you're staying here. Not moving. You'll still be next door when we come back in the summer."

"Mmmm."

"You and Clare are friends again."

Binny nodded.

"I wish Max could teleport or something! I'll make him Skype you."

"It's not just Max."

"Oh." Gareth took off his glasses and rubbed them the way he did when he felt awkward.

"I suppose I'd better stop telling people you're my girlfriend, hadn't I?"

"You don't have to if it helps."

"It does help," said Gareth, and stopped fumbling

with his glasses to glance at her face. Their eyes met, startled, as if they had just seen something new and astonishing.

"Bin," said Gareth, and all at once he gathered her up, much as he had gathered up the pigeon: easily, as if it was the obvious thing to do.

"Burnt toast," said Binny, sniffing, burrowed in his jacket.

"Seaweed," he replied, and she could feel his laughter as he spoke.

"Why . . . ?"

But there was no time for why. Voices were calling from both their houses, "Binny? Binny? Gareth?"

Binny sighed and gave one last hug. Gareth untangled his face from her hair, pushed on his glasses, and was transformed into his bony, untouchable self.

"What about the pigeon? Are you coming? I'm letting it fly in a few minutes."

"I'll watch from my roof."

They both spoke as if nothing had happened. As if their hearts were not beating slightly faster than before. As if they hadn't noticed how the place where they were standing had suddenly tipped a little closer to the sun.

James appeared.

"Hello! Don't . . ."

"We weren't going to," said Gareth. "Were we, Bin? Were you going to kiss James?"

"I . . . No! Of course I wasn't!"

"Neither was I," said Gareth, with such a sudden wicked gleam in his eyes that James became suspicious and demanded, "What's funny? What are you laughing at? Tell me what's funny?"

Binny left Gareth to deal with him and escaped to her attic.

Now she was perched on her father's desk, head and shoulders out of the window, elbows resting on the new tiles of the roof, so high up that she could see clearly into Gareth's garden as well as her own and Miss Piper's. She was surrounded by birds. The local pigeons were fast learners when it came to finding food. There was a flurry of wings as Gareth opened his kitchen door and then they were down searching for seeds within seconds of them being scattered. Binny saw Gareth's pigeon flutter from his hands to join them. It merged with the others so completely that if it had not been white it would have been lost amongst the flock. It flew with them when the food was finished and they rose to settle on the roofs once more. It was well again.

"Perfect!" called Binny, clapping, and Gareth saw her looking down at him and waved triumphantly back. Then he went inside, but Binny stayed on her rooftop, listening.

Sounds floated upward.

Out of sight, on the street below, the two cars

belonging to Gareth's family were being slowly loaded. Voices rose, so clear in the bright air, that she could tell every one. There was a great deal of conversation, mostly the organizing kind, about keys and distances and flower tubs to be watered, but also "Congratulations! Oh, how lovely!"

and

"Most dogs travel in the back and put up with it!"

and

"A warm day at last and we have to go!"

Also

"That is absolute rubbish! Absolutely not art! I thought you'd got rid of it! Take it out of the car at once!"

Gareth and Max, Clem and James, Gareth's father and stepmother (Binny remembered with gratitude her hot chocolate and kindness). A welcoming shriek for James told her that Dill was there too, and so was Miss Piper, her witch voice lapping like water against stone.

In a few minutes, Binny thought, I will go down and smile at her to show I'm not witched, and I'll then say good-bye to Gareth and Max. It will be all right, not terrible, because it's nearly summer. Soon they'll be back for weeks and weeks. And then when they're gone I'll walk into town and wait for the bank to open at nine. I'll be the first one in.

Binny had dressed that morning much more carefully than usual. Pink striped shirt, comfy old jeans, seaweed hair tied up in a knot. She was ready and waiting, up on the roof. Bright sky, red tiles, and a racing wind that whipped the sea, "the glinting tinfoil sea," murmured Binny, "into chains of foam right up to the horizon."

She thought, I'm going to write that down.

She had brought Clare's pen up to the roof with her, and her precious blue and silver notebook was on the desk below. She stooped to pick it up, and then looked for a long time at the picture on the cover.

The Little Prince with his birds to help him fly, his rose and his sheep and his active volcano.

L'essential est invisible pour les yeux.

What is most important is invisible to the eyes.

"Hello Dad," said Binny softly, and felt in the sunlight on her shoulders the comradeship of storytellers.

What had Clare said? *I thought you'd like a pen because you're a writer.*

Yes I am, agreed Binny, and unsnapped the silver elastic around the notebook.

The pages fell open as if they had been waiting for that moment and inside was the missing money.

Then the wind stopped blowing and the sea was stilled. *Bang, bang, bang* went Binny's shocked and thankful heart, hammering into silence every sound in the town. For a while it was as if she had slipped through one of her gaps in the world into a new and empty place.

In that place there was nothing but air and silence, and the feeling of dry leaves under her hands.

She found her eyes were closed.

When she opened them the money was still there.

This time she counted it, counted it twice, with shaky fingers.

Two hundred pounds.

Found.

Found! thought Binny, and was back in the world again, up on the roof, listening to the sounds of the cars being packed next door, waiting for the ache of saying good-bye to Max, feeling the warmth of the sun on the tiles, hearing a new voice, Clare, calling, "Hello! Where's Binny?"

"Wuff!" barked Max in greeting.

Somebody was whistling, just out of sight.

Binny held tight to the money.

Max barked again, startling a flurry of pigeons to clatter upward into the sky.

Time was turning backward.

Slate blue, earth brown, and white, the pigeons rose from the eaves and roofs, rattling wings and a rush of air as they circled over the street.

A gasping shriek of dismay, worried cries, and then suddenly a door banged shut.

"Miss Piper!" cried voices: Clem, Binny's mother, Gareth's stepmother, and Clare.

"How can anyone be that frightened of pigeons?"

That was Gareth, and then James, high and clear.

"Here's her bag that she dropped! It's all bursted open!"

"Let me knock! Oh she's heard me."

"Miss Piper, you worried us!"

"Miss Piper!"

"Miss Piper!"

Miss Piper.

At last Binny understood. How the money had come to be abandoned, and by whom, and the reason why . . .

"Here!" she shouted. "It's here! It's here!" and she leaped from the desk, flew the attic stairs, jumped the house stairs, and hurtled through the front door, rushed to Miss Piper, and pushed the notes into her hands.

"I'm sorry! I'm sorry! I didn't know! I lost it, it was awful! I truly didn't mean to take it. I'm sorry, I'm so sorry, I'm truly sorrier than sorry. I promise . . ."

Miss Piper's face showed not a trace of emotion as she took the notes and folded them. She gave no sign of having heard a word. Binny stammered to a halt and then stood twisting her empty hands more and more uncomfortably under the chill of the calm blue gaze.

"So you had it after all," said Miss Piper, in her smooth, lapping water, lipstick pink voice. "Yes Binny. Just as I guessed."

Chapter Twenty
* * *
Afterward

There were no secrets left. Nothing was hidden. So far as anyone could tell, there were no gaps in the world through which things might slip and be lost. Gareth was gone and Max was gone. Later that Friday morning Clare had had the idea of rushing Binny to the market for apologizing pink tulips to give to Miss Piper. Binny had chosen them and carried them with anxious carefulness. Miss Piper had received them without surprise.

(Was there somewhere, Binny had wondered when she was safely back home, a peg doll Binny, holding a bunch of pink flowers?)

("Probably," said Clare.)

* * *

Days passed, and the wind grew warm. There was often a white pigeon dozing in the roof corners. When Binny looked out of her skylight it would glance at her and blink. The blink said, "Yes. I believe we did meet before."

In Binny's attic they at last found a home for their father's bag. It stood tucked between the wall and the desk, very much as it had done in the olden days, and it had become a place for small and precious things. James had begun this, searching for a hiding place for his two fallen out top teeth. "Dill is *not* having them for his collection!" he explained, winding them round and round with sticky tape, and Binny had promised that they would be safe. When Clem heard about this she handed over a small brown envelope, her first week's earnings after the café reopened. "Don't give it to me, however much I beg!" she told Binny. "It's for end-of-the-world emergencies!"

Binny herself had put Max's puppy collar in the bag, just because it seemed the perfect place to keep it, and then, very recently, her mother had come up the attic stairs with a tiny square box in a padded envelope. "You can look if you like," she told Binny.

"It's all right," Binny reassured her, hugging her. "It really is. I don't need to look."

Elsewhere in the house, things were coming back into place. The spirit level had been returned to the living room mantelpiece. Pete was often in the kitchen or round about the house. He'd come whistling up the street and they'd rush to the door. Binny wrote and wrote and wrote. She wrote till she'd unburdened the story of the money, and her mind was all untangled and her thoughts ran clear again.

"It's summer!" she said to Clare one day, and it was.

James and Dill were in the garden, although only James was visible. Dill was in the apple tree. He was looking rather thoughtful and holding very tight. James thought he must be stuck but Dill shook his head. He was not yet prepared to say he had no hope of getting down. Not to James, who scampered the branches like a sunny, energetic squirrel.

"Shall I tell you what to do?" inquired James.

"No thank you."

"Why not?"

"You're six," said Dill, so witheringly James bounced in indignation, dislodged Dill from his branch, and landed him in the grass.

"Told you I wasn't stuck," said Dill, smiling his downward smile.

Clare said dreamily, "Yes, it's definitely summer. Listen to Clem."

Clem's flute was climbing and climbing, echoing, glass clear into the high blue sky, startling the dozing pigeons, spiraling up amongst the seagulls, echoing over the red roofs and the marketplace, reaching toward the harbor and the lighthouse on the rocks far out to sea.

"I shouldn't mind playing a flute," said Clare, admiring but yawning. "Not all the practicing that Clem does, I don't mean. Just now and then, to surprise people. Only the trouble is, I don't like music. I'd always rather it was turned off. I wonder if anyone likes it really, or do they just pretend . . . What are you writing?"

Binny scribbled a minute longer, and then showed her.

"I shouldn't mind playing a flute," said Clare, yawning. "Not all the practicing that Clem does, I don't mean. Just now and then, to surprise people. Only the trouble is, I don't like music. I'd always rather it was turned off. I wonder if anyone likes it really, or do they just pretend . . . What are you writing?"

Clare read it out loud, as well as she could for laughing, and asked, "How did you do that?"

"It's something I've discovered. Writing down exactly what people say. Then you really hear them, just as they are. It's one of those half magics, like Miss Piper's peg dolls."

"Miss Piper," said Clare, "is not a witch. The peg dolls, Pete's van, the little dog she gave you to remind you that you were in her power, that broomstick, they are all ordinary things. You just want her to be a witch to be exciting."

"Of course I do," agreed Binny. Now that she was out of the direct line of Miss Piper's witchy ways, her thoughts sparkled with interest. Who would not want to live next door to a witch, however complaining, however nosy, however pink and purple flowery . . .

No one was more disappointed than Binny when, as silently as Miss Piper had arrived, she was suddenly no longer there.

Binny discovered this one midsummer morning, on a day when the Cornwallis household was even busier than usual. They had gone to bed far too late, and got up far too early, and Clem's list of things that had to be done was still far from complete. Yet Binny was in her attic, in her favorite position, half in and half out of the skylight window, untangling her thoughts.

She left behind, wrote Binny, who had peered through the letterbox, *her butterfly doormat, her picture of the Queen aged seven, the honesty leaves in their little pot, and all the pretend flowers in her windows. But when you look past the windows, the rooms are bare. You can see all the spellbooks are gone from the shelves, and as well, last night when it was black black dark, I heard the strangest noise on the tiles overhead. . . .*

A great whirling scraping right over my head . . .

"Binny!" yelled Clem from downstairs.

. . . and that huge black broomstick . . .

"Come on Binny!" shouted James. "Come on! Come on! Even Gertie and Pecker are ready!"

. . . that she never used to sweep with . . .

"Binny, Bin, Belinda, Bel!" called her mother.

. . . *has* . . .

"Do you want to be a bridesmaid," demanded Clem, "or not?"

. . . *vanished!* scribbled Binny, and ran.

Turn the page for a
sneak peek at *Love to Everyone*

"AND WHAT WILL YOU DO WITH YOURSELF WHILE your brother's laid up?" Clarry's grandfather asked her.

"I thought I might learn to swim," said Clarry, and he burst out laughing and said, "Ha, ha, very good!" and later told her grandmother that she was "quite a little character!" as if she had proposed to take up golf or arranging the flowers in church.

However, Clarry was quite serious. For a long time she had envied the boys their swimming. They went almost every day.

"Well, you're a girl and they are boys," Clarry's grandmother had said when Clarry first mentioned it, a year or two before, and at the time Clarry had nodded, disappointed but accepting. There were a lot of things to accept, she found, about the differences between girls and boys. That boys had pocket money and girls didn't. That boys needed to learn things at school but girls just had to be quietly occupied. That Peter had a bicycle and could ride all over town, but that her own boundaries were school (two minutes' walk away) and Miss Vane's house (across the road).

And most of all, that the boys knew best. And boys were best. It was fact. It was life. It was natural history.

Rupert had learned to swim when he was eight, in the concrete tank at boarding school (unheated gray water, six feet deep, straight in and no shrieking). Every boy in the school learned to swim; it was the only sensible thing to do, the alternative being to drown.

After the school swimming tank, the buoyant blue and green waters off the Cornish coast were easy. A foaming translucent element of liquid airy joy.

Rupert, on a hot summer's day, would leave his grandparents' house to run across field and moor, racing along narrow fox paths between bramble and gorse, and galloping quaggy stretches of bog. Not pausing for thorns, nor the fiery patches his sandshoes rubbed on his heels, shoving aside fat sheep, to where the cliff dipped down to the sea. Here, high tide or low, there was always water. In the last few yards of his race, he shed shirt and shoes, and when he reached the edge he leaped without pausing. Each time it was the best moment of life. One element to another. One world to another. Escape.

It was not the same for Peter. Even before he broke his leg, he wasn't much of a runner. The first time he saw Rupert leap from the cliff he assumed his cousin would drown. He shuffled to the edge and peered over, down into the blue water. There was Rupert, only a few feet below him, laughing and blowing like a human porpoise.

"Come on!" called Rupert.

Every now and then Peter was struck by a mood of reckless madness. It hit him then. He also dragged off his clothes and, in a skinny tangle of shoulders and shinbones, hit the rocking water. Peter could swim too; twice a week in summer term the boys from his day school were marched down to the town pool. In water Peter was as agile as Rupert. He could dive as well. He was the first to take off from the cliff in a swooping header, but it was Rupert who had said, the year before, "We should bring Clarry."

"She can't swim," said Peter.

"She'd soon learn, like we did."

Clarry, when asked, said, "Yes! Yes, please! But how could I? What would I wear?"

They looked blank.

"What do you wear?"

"Bathing suits or we don't bother."

"I can't not bother and I haven't got a bathing suit," said Clarry.

"Ask Grandmother," suggested Rupert, but that was no use. Clarry's grandmother said that little girls paddled. They paddled in their summer dresses carefully at the water's edge, having left their shoes and stockings neatly on a rock. This behavior entirely prevented any risk of drowning, said Clarry's grandmother, and closed the sitting-room door.

Clarry (in private) contemplated her reflection in her knickers and her liberty bodice. It was awful. She tried on Peter's old bathing suit and it hung in great black loops from her shoulders to her knees. And so she gave up hope of swimming with the boys that year, although she often sat on the cliff above, watching as they dived and porpoised through the blue and green water.

And then the next summer, there was the sovereign!

It was agony to part with, but she did it, and for ten shillings bought a black bathing suit from a dismal little shop near the marketplace. It was made of wool, rather rubbed up because it was not new, baggy around her knees, and gathered with large bright blue bows at the shoulders. Clarry didn't like the bows, but the bathing suit was the lightest thing she had ever worn. She put it on and pranced into Peter's room, saying, "Look! Look! Look!"

Peter was lying on his bed, reading and resting his aching leg. He put down his book and peered at her. He said, "It's the worst thing I've ever seen you wearing."

"Oh," said Clarry. "It can't be!"

"It is. Can you get that blue ribbon muck off?"

"The bows? They're what hold it on."

"Well, it's awful," said Peter, picking up his book again. "Wait till Rupe sees it. He'll tell you."

"What'll I tell her?" asked Rupert, coming in just then. "Oh . . ."

He walked away across the room and looked out of the window for a minute before turning round and saying, "Superb!"

"Are you mad?" asked Peter. "Look at her!"

"I only wanted to learn to swim," said Clarry humbly. "I'm tired of just paddling. I know it's not a very nice swimming suit."

"It's just right," said Rupert. "Come on, then! Put something on top and we'll try it out. We'll run across the moor."

Clarry cheered up tremendously, pulled a dress on top of the bathing suit, hugged Peter good-bye, and scampered after Rupert so quickly that in less than twenty minutes they were at the cliff edge, looking down.

"Now what?" asked Clarry.

"Jump!"

"Straight in, not round by the rocks?"

"No, no, of course not! You said you were tired of paddling!"

"Is that what you did the first time you went swimming? Jump straight in?"

"Yes. Straight in, and no screaming at the cold or else detention in the gym!"

"And then you just started swimming, as easily as that?"

"Of course," said Rupert, and he honestly believed it was true.

"It's not far down, is it?"

"Hardly a step," said Rupert. "In you go and you'll come up swimming like a duckling. Even Pete did. I'll count you down, shall I?"

Clarry wavered on the brink, nearly overbalancing.

"Three . . . two . . . don't try diving. Diving needs practice. Do it the safe way, feet first, just to start with. Now then, one!"

The safe way, Rupert had said, and Clarry shut her eyes, stepped into nothingness, flailed in sudden panic, and then found herself plunging, down and down below the slapping green waves, into such coldness that she gasped in great panicky gulps, not air, but salt water.

Everything ended then, the whole warm lovely world gone in a moment. There was no direction to reach for, and no air to breathe.

There was an icy grip, disbelief, and then blackness.

Rupert, smiling, waited for her to bob up.

This did not happen. Nothing happened. The green glass sea swung and rippled, quite undisturbed. Rupert shaded his eyes and craned sideways to see if she was climbing up by the rocks, and as he did so, he caught sight of a small black shadow rocking in the depths.

Sheet lightning fear flashed from the water, blinding Rupert as he dived. Even so, he found her, weightless as a shadow, dragged her to the surface, towed her to the rocks, rolled her over, and hit her between her shoulders.

Water poured from Clarry in streams and rivers and fountains. She was fish cold and gray granite pale.

"Clarry!" bellowed Rupert, and turned her upside down and shook her. She retched and came alive but her eyes didn't open.

Rupert picked her up, hung her over his shoulder, staggered across the rocks, up the steep sandy path, and lowered her onto the turf. He wrapped his shirt round her, rubbed her back, and shouted at her. When he propped her up she slid sideways, heavy now, and limp as a jellyfish.

"Oh, God, Clarry," moaned Rupert, and saw her reach out a hand to comfort him.

After a few minutes, she began shaking and then crying

silently, yet more salt water pouring down her cold cheeks.

"Why didn't you swim?" demanded Rupert, suddenly angry, but she only shivered and cried even more.

"Poor little duckling," said Rupert, and at last Clarry sat up and wiped her eyes.

It took him ages to get her home. She kept stopping to lean on things. When they finally arrived he left her in the hall and knocked on the sitting-room door.

This time, the grandparents were not so calm as usual. Twice in one summer was too much. First Peter, now this. It beggared belief. Every year their grandchildren were met at the station, provided with beds, and catered for with astonishing quantities of food. There was sea and moorland, a town, a garden, and a pony. What more could be expected? Where was their common sense? Why on earth couldn't Rupert be trusted to take care of Clarry?

"It wasn't his fault," croaked Clarry, the first words she had spoken.

"Never heard such nonsense!" growled her grandfather, and Rupert was sent off to fetch the doctor while Clarry was hustled up to bed in the room next to Peter's, piled with blankets, and scolded.

"What's happened? What's happened? What's happened?" demanded Peter. They closed his bedroom door tight shut because they had enough to deal with as it was, and then they opened it again because he was thumping on the wall. With the help of his crutches, Peter dragged himself out of bed and went to join the turmoil in the room next door.

"She might have drowned!" fumed her grandfather. "A nice job for me, that would have been, telling her father she'd drowned!"

Peter snorted and said something so outrageous that he was ordered to get out. The doctor arrived, with Rupert in tow. Clarry fell unhelpfully asleep in the middle of him listening to her lungs. She slept for hours and hours. When she woke up her grandmother was sitting beside her looking terribly bored.

"I'm sorry," said Clarry.

Her grandmother looked down at her.

"I shouldn't have jumped. I guessed that really. I just thought . . . I thought . . ."

"Rupert must know best," finished her grandmother.

Clarry nodded.

Now you know he didn't, said her grandmother, not in words, but with an eloquent sniff. She gave another sniff as she picked up the sodden bundle of Clarry's bathing suit from the washstand. "Is that what you spent your birthday money on? What a dreadful-looking garment!"

"It didn't take all the money," said Clarry. "Don't throw it away. I need it."

"I can't imagine what for."

"I'm still going to learn to swim."

"Oh, are you?"

"Yes, and I heard what Peter said. Father would have minded if I'd drowned!"

"Everyone would have minded, Peter most of all," said her grandmother sharply. She got up to go then, but hesitated at the door, and then suddenly came back, stooped, and kissed the top of Clarry's head.

"You should go to sleep again now."

Clarry dropped off almost at once, but she woke in the night gasping with fear and groping blindly into the blackness surrounding her. For a day or two, it hurt her chest to breathe. It rained, and she stayed in her room, reading Sherlock Holmes adventures in faded blue paper-covered copies of The Strand Magazine. Her grandfather had produced them, silent proof that he too was glad she had not drowned. On the third day she felt better, the sun came out, and her grandmother handed her the bathing suit, dried out and transformed. The saggy legs had been shortened and edged with neat black bands, the blue bows on the shoulders replaced with black and white ruffles, and all the seams taken in. Most surprising of all, her grandmother had news for her. She said, "I have been asking my friends. I find that one of them has a grown-up daughter who swims. Also she tells me that there is a part of the bay that is roped off for safe bathing. Would you like me to arrange for you to meet?"

So in time Clarry learned to swim after all, and later to dive, not like a duckling but like a slim black seal. Rupert said, "See! I knew you could do it!" and Peter said, "You shouldn't have panicked. Swimming is obvious."

"Swimming is not obvious!" said Clarry. "Not unless you're a fish. Or frog. Otherwise it's a lot of puffing and managing. Arms as well as legs. And hair in your eyes and being absolutely drenched. Not just wet, absolutely . . . oh, well, it doesn't matter. I can do it now anyway."

The boys were moderately pleased with her. They were never very good at admitting they were wrong, but she carried on adoring them just the same.

Looking for another great book?
Find it
IN THE MIDDLE.

Fun, fantastic books for kids
in the in-be**TWEEN** age.

IntheMiddleBooks.com

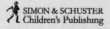

For Binny it had happened the same way people become friends. Totally. Inevitable from the beginning. Only it was not friends; it was enemies.

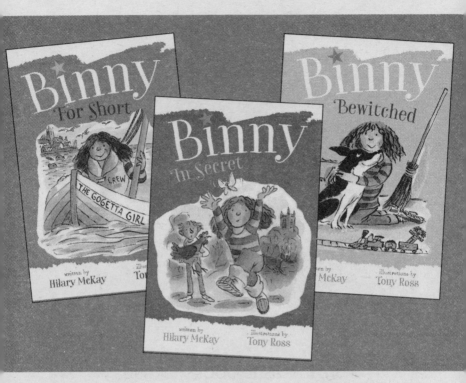

★"A well-crafted story that balances moments of hilarity with poignancy."
—*Publishers Weekly*, starred review for *Binny for Short*

★"The writing is gorgeous, clear as water; the characters vivid and lively; the story so real each moment of loss, fear, delight, and love absolutely visceral."
—*Kirkus Reviews*, starred review for *Binny for Short*

★"McKay continues to enthrall readers with her vigorous blend of screwball comedy and heartfelt emotion."
—*Horn Book*, starred review for *Binny in Secret*

★"There's never a dull moment in the Cornwallis household— nor one not rich with love and laughter."
—*Kirkus Reviews*, starred review for *Binny in Secret*

PRINT AND EBOOK EDITIONS AVAILABLE
From Margaret K. McElderry Books   simonandschuster.com/kids